The Gate of Limbo

Chronicles of the Grigori

Book One

by

Donovan M. Neal

Scriptures marked KJV are taken from the KING JAMES VERSION (KJV): KING JAMES
VERSION, public domain.

Ordering Information:
Quantity sales. Special discounts are available on quantity purchases by corporations, associations and others. For details, contact the publisher at the email above.

Printed in the United States of America

ISBN 9781670007483 (Print Version)

Dedication

I dedicate this book to those who dare to dream and see it through to completion. May your imagination ever lead you to new realms.

Scriptures

Genesis 50:20 But as for you, ye thought evil against me; but God meant it unto good, to bring to pass, as it is this day, to save much people alive.

Romans 9:19 Thou wilt say then unto me, Why doth he yet find fault? For who hath resisted his will?

Romans 8:29 For whom he did foreknow, he also did predestinate to be conformed to the image of his Son, that he might be the first-born among many brethren.

Romans 8:30 Moreover whom he did predestinate, them he also called: and whom he called, them he also justified: and whom he justified, them he also glorified.

"When you pray for Hitler and Stalin how do you actually teach yourself to make the prayer real? The two things that help me are (a) A continual grasp of the idea that one is only joining one's feeble little voice to the perpetual intercession of Christ who died for these very men. (b) A recollection, as firm as I can make it, of all one's own cruelty; which might have blossomed under different conditions into something terrible. You and I are not at bottom so different from these ghastly creatures." -- C.S. Lewis, Letters (1951)

Acknowledgments

To the Lord Jesus Christ, who loves me.

To my children: Candace, Christopher and Alexander–you can do great things!

To the authors, comic books artists and authors, comic books artists, and writers who have come before, and who unknowingly have breathed on the embers of my imagination.

To all my beta readers and friends who shared both critiques and encouragement.

To my wife Nettie, who cheered me on when I had nothing and said, "Wow!" after reading the prologue of my first novel.

May God truly bless you all.

Chapter One

In the beginning…

Henel James was excited to be traveling to Heaven. Yeshua had granted permission to ascend to the Heavenly Jerusalem and to meet with the chief of the Grigoric order of angels: Argoth Chief of Eyes and Sephiroth. Andel was waiting for him at the Orphanic transport point.

"I see you are ever rushed to get to your destination. Are you ready to leave Adamson?" spoke Andel.

Argoth had assigned Andel to prepare him to understand the ways of angels. And the angel had been a great assist in helping the world's human population understand the motivations and designs of the celestials: the term non-raptured humans called angels. The Jerusalem Post was voracious in its desire to provide content to its readers, and Henel James was its premier reporter. He was on the scene when Enoch and Elijah first arrived in Jerusalem. He was also there when they were killed by the Anti-Christ and former Chancellor of Earth: Leto Alexander. Henel always made it a point to sniff out and to be at the center of a story.

And now a member of an angelic royal house of the Grigori invited him to tour the greatest library ever created and interview him. Henel was both excited and anxious for the opportunity. Ever since Yeshua had returned, He had established the reconstruction of the world's political structures, economy, and the delivery of goods and services had been underway now for fifty years. Not soon after the Lord Yeshua had arrived, Henel had made the acquaintance of Argoth the Chief of all Grigori. The angel had made it clear that he possessed a story he thought would interest the reporter. Henel was elated, thinking to himself that he could gain an exclusive that might lead to a Nobel Prize.

But that was almost fifty years ago now.

It took Henel a while to understand that celestials possessed a very different concept of time than earth-born humans were used to. Celestials were never rushed and possessed little concept of immediacy; unlike those whose life-spans had in the past been measured in decades and who still held to what was now outdated ideas about time. No one on Earth had died for fifty years and Henel was still wrapping his head around the concept he too would live forever.

When the word had arrived that Argoth requested his presence, Henel gave word to Andel and rushed to the Orphanic portal

2

that would take him to Heaven. Here, he would meet his friend and finally see what all the fuss about taking this angelic means of transportation. A mode of transport that would allow him to pass from the material realm of men to the spiritual realm of Heaven.

Humph, I'm going to Heaven and, I am not even dead. Who'd a thunk it? He thought to himself.

Henel looked up into the sky and breathed hard and replied to his friend. "Alright. Let's do this before I change my mind."

"Brace yourself, my friend. Orphanic travel can be disorientating for the first time."

Henel brushed him off and replied, "I'm sure it will be fine, let's go."

Henel had traveled all over the world; from Antarctica to the Amazon jungles. He had been embedded with military operations when the Americans invaded Taiwan during the Sino/American seven day war. He was an accomplished pilot and had parachuted out of planes to reach remote locations. He felt comfortable in his ability to finally experience this method of transportation.

Andel smiled knowingly, "As you wish." The angel then uttered the Elomic command to summon a ladder.

Henel understood the mechanics of how the ladder worked. An Ophanim materialized over the summoned area and then used their bodies to create a dimensional wake that lifted the summoner within the cavitation the creature made. Essentially, the creature pulled the traveler through dimensions where it deposited its rider wherever the recipient desired.

Andel briefed Henel on what to expect and as promised; a prismatic funnel cloud appeared over the two and all around him, the colors of the rainbow enveloped him in light and a sudden sound like that of an aircraft engine taking off; saturated his hearing. His ears popped, and he felt the urge to yawn to equalize the pressure in his head cavity.

He looked down at his feet and realized that they had lifted from the ground and as quick as he had noted he was levitating; Andel and he jetted upwards into the sky at a fantastic rate of speed. He watched as he left the environs of the blue planet of earth and the blackness of space rushed forward to embrace them. The moon dashed past him and his eyes watched in fascination as Mars soared into view and quickly ran past him rearward. Particles of space debris struck the funnel cloud and he could feel a jarring turbulence as they jetted through the solar system's asteroid belt. Jupiter raced past with its red eye spinning larger than the earth itself, and it captivated Henel. He suddenly felt as if someone had placed a giant weight on his breast as he noted that they seemed to accelerate as they under-flew the rings of Saturn. Henel's eyes grew wide as they left behind the solar system and their pace sped up the more, as stars and multicolored gas clouds burst into view then as quickly vanished into the distance.

He suddenly started to hyperventilate.

"Breathe Henel. Breathe." Andel said.

But the sensation was overwhelming. The vertigo of moving so fast spun around the knowledge he was in the depths of space passing through what could only be the Milky Way. Suddenly the galaxy that was his home was just one of several, then hundreds, then millions and the scale of what he saw caused his mind to reel at what he beheld. The Ophanim turned and when he turned, Andel and Henel turned, and Henel reached out to grab Andel's arm to stabilize the human, for the dizziness overtook him.

Henel hyperventilated the more. His eyes widened as they approached the accretion disc of a gigantic black hole. Henel had seen them on television, read about them in books but now he was face to face with the phenomena and he was both awed and grew ever fearful. Faster they moved and closer the pull of the giant gravity well caused the funnel to shake and the G-forces made Henel's face to contort slightly, and he cried out in concern.

"I can't... breathe... my chest."

Andel nodded. "We are almost there it will pass. Try to just breathe."

Into blackness they flew, piercing the center of the black hole and the vision of Henel was such that even his eyes felt like they would fall into the back of his head. His tongue pressed hard against the roof of his mouth and his teeth gritted while his hands shook.

Screams and wails pierced the sound of the roaring funnel cloud. Henel strained his eyes to see in the distance, flickering lights, flames, and a great lake-like dimension was within the black hole. The sounds of screams and the echoes of anguish pierced his hearing, and he strained to lift his hands to cover his ears and he too opened his mouth to scream. The gravitational pressure was crushing and he let out a low moan that grew into a cry for help.

A bright light then suddenly flashed over them and the funnel cloud was gone. Henel was on his knees screaming and taking in large gulps of air.

He looked up with Andel standing over him shaking his

head, and the angel said, "Thank you for flying the friendly skies." He chuckled as Henel's eyebrow raised and he pursed his lips in annoyance and replied. "Ha, ha. Come on, let's go see this library of yours."

Henel stood to his feet and dusted himself off and the two headed towards the fabled Grigoric Hall of Records: creation's greatest library.

* * *

Henel walked upon streets of gold and he was fascinated by all that was around him. The colors were more brilliant than anything than he had ever seen. It was as if they traveled through the most vibrant three dimensional painting. The smell was sweet, and the air was clear.

"Welcome to my home Henel James; though it is marvelous. Imagine what it will be like after El creates a new Heaven and a new Earth! Creation is to be renewed! We live in exciting times!"

Henel nodded. He had never witnessed Heaven. It was fiction told by Christians and or Jews who believed in El. It was the dwelling place of the Father. The capital of the universe. Henel had heard many a redeemed man and woman talk about it. None had words to describe it. Those men and women who had not been given glorified bodies but had survived the return of Yeshua had not seen the dimension. Henel was one of the few allowed to witness it.

He walked around in awe. He raised his phone to capture images and Andel stopped him.

"No Adamson, do not do it, for you walk on holy ground. The things you see are not for entertainment, but to glorify God. There are things your electronic devices cannot capture. If you try, your image will wash out. Even the air is alive here in Heaven; do not stir a desire for it to restrict your lungs for being profane."

Henel looked at Andel and replied, "The air is alive?"

"Yes Adamson, all of Heaven is alive. It is my charge to see you to and from Heaven's shores safely. There is a risk for you to be here when your flesh has not yet been redeemed. The air itself could attack you as a virus if not for the restraining will of Yeshua's seal over you. But fear not, you are safe, but I would advise you to not push the limits of God's grace. You may record the interview. But do not photograph what you see."

Henel nodded, "Is this it?"

8

Andel now nodded and replied, "Aye, the Great Library. Come."

The building shimmered as a mirage. Great steps flowed towards it and the two made their way up translucent golden steps towards giant golden doors gilded with silver. Something akin to marble columns lined the entryway, and the two walked in. From floor to ceiling the building was abuzz with life.

"Are all these Grigori?" asked Henel.

"Yes, the Grigori here are the curators of the library. They see to its well being and to content collection."

"What knowledge is in here?" Henel asked.

"Everything," replied Andel.

"What do you mean everything?"

Andel hunched his shoulders and repeated himself. "Everything," replied Andel.

"So, if I wanted to know who shot John F. Kennedy that information is in here?"

Andel paused, "If the assassination of an ancient leader of your tribe is the only thing that springs to your mind in terms of what could be found in this storehouse of knowledge, I must admit that the limits of your curiosity would disappoint me. But yes, the knowledge is here."

Henel became suddenly still, and he eyed the vast number of books that existed in the building. Countless attendants hurried about placing new books and pulling older tomes from various stacks of golden plated cases. Each wooden bookcase was ten feet high and chains were attached to all the books. The building held multiple levels that extended as far as the eye could see and Grigori floated from one level to another to read and to attend to the tomes. Each was locked with a padlock and others were free to be removed. Golden pairs of eyes decored draping banners that hung throughout the room.

"Excuse me sir," said Henel. "May I have a word with you?"

Henel went to reach out and tap the shoulder of the attendant, and Andel quickly grabbed him and spun him around. "Do it not! You risk dissolution. Do not interfere with the Grigori, to do so risks altering reality itself! They handle the word of God. And IT must NOT be interfered with; do you understand me?"

Henel was shaken by the force with which Andel used towards him and nodded silently.

"You are my friend Henel James. I would very much not like to have you be the first human to die in fifty years."

"Thank you," Henel replied. No longer sure of sure what he walked into by agreeing to interview Argoth.

The reporter for the Jerusalem Post continued his observation of the activity of those within the building and noted that all attendants had keys, and various sections of the library were numbered in angelic script: script which Henel found that he could understand.

"Are those... years?" asked Henel.

"Aye," replied Andel. "Those are the dates used to denote the passage of time."

Henel looked closer, "But those dates seem to predate the existence of man..."

Andel cut him off and replied, "You will undoubtedly have many questions Henel. Argoth will be best equipped to answer them."

Henel nodded and said, "Is it me, or does this place seem much larger than what it appears outside?"

Andel smiled, "That is because it is Adamson."

"How is that possible?" asked Henel.

"All things are possible with God, Adamson. The Hall of Records exists within two dimensions. One you can see and another that is infinite. When you passed into the Hall, you passed into another dimension. Here, all things are stored and nothing is lost. This is the repository of all Grigori. When they complete the charge of documenting a tome, it is brought here, cataloged and housed. There will come a day in which the books will be opened and a time when the living and the dead shall be judged from what is written within."

Henel tilted his head to the side in curiosity, "Judgment? Is *more* judgment coming?"

Andel scowled, "Have you no knowledge of the tome the Lord God has given your people?"

And I saw the dead, small and great, stand before God; and the books were opened: and another book was opened, which is the book of life: and the dead were judged out of those things which were written in the books, according to their works.

"There are those who have perished: both human and angel that... we shall see again."

Andel escorted Henel into a room that glowed. He motioned for the man to go forward.

Henel chuckled, "Don't go in the liiight!"

Andel looked upon him blankly. "Argoth awaits you inside."

"You are not coming in?"

"No," said Andel. "The words of the Chief of Eyes are for you and you alone. I will wait here until you are done."

Henel turned and looked at the glowing door, then stepped through the light.

Chapter Two

Argoth stood looking out a window as he waited for Henel to arrive. He had watched the human his entire life and had studied his tome. Argoth knew that inevitably, they would meet. Both were chroniclers of their worlds; both seekers of knowledge.

Henel James walked into the light-filled room. The ornate walls were filled with books and stained glass windows. Great flames, lit torches, and mirrors adorned the ceiling and reflected light throughout the room.

Argoth turned and smiled at the human, "Greetings, Henel son of James. Please, may I offer you refreshment?"

Henel returned his smile. "Thank you Mr. Argoth; that would be delightful."

Argoth frowned, "Please… just call me Argoth. I have seen that you enjoy the fruit of the vine. Here try this." Argoth waved his hand and a golden goblet appeared in front of Henel and smelled of grapes.

He reached for the goblet suspended in the air and the aroma was sweet, and he allowed the drink to touch his lips and savored it. "Goodness, what is this? It's extraordinary!"

Argoth laughed, "It is wine, and the grapes taken from the fields of Elysium and mixed with the leaves of Mirabel. I am glad you enjoy it. Please let us be seated. I'm sure you have many questions you wish to ask me."

Henel walked towards a couch and the two sat across from one another and Henel spoke, "Is it permitted to record our conversation?"

Argoth looked puzzled and asked, "Do you not have a pen and paper?"

"I do," replied Henel. "But my recorder will be allowing me to capture the fullness of your story and for me to give you my undivided attention."

Argoth nodded, "I understand. But you should be aware that your device will not function as you expect in my presence. I suggest if you desire to capture my words you stick to pen and paper. But you may find that after we speak, you may not desire to share my words."

Now it was Henel's turn to look at his interviewee puzzled, "Why not?"

"Because Henel James, the words I speak are words that are

both before the fall of Lucifer, and after. They are the stuff of legend, and to those who do not understand the origins of the celestial war will not understand. Even now there are humans who despite what their eyes can see, view Yeshua as but a foreign invader. This corruption of the mind will fester and grow for a thousand years until it will be cut out by the King of Hosts. Then He will raise up all that ever was. Then shall the books be opened, but it will be too late; for those who will hear the reading thereof will be subject to the second death and thrown alive into the Lake of Fire, and then Henel James... then it will be too late."

Henel took out his pen, clicked the top, and the point revealed from its shaft and he quickly began to scribble notes.

"I have learned that in heaven, during the final battle before the Horde was ejected, there arose in the sky a shattering. As if a glass had been cracked and all that could be seen were multiple versions of themselves fighting: multiple realities. Is this true?"

Argoth nodded, "The thing is as you say."

Henel scribbled quickly on his notepad and continued. "If I am predestined to be here, are we not but a pawn in God's game? Who can resist his will if He has seen and orchestrated the outcome of all things? How can any of us be judged if such were the case?

16

There are readers on Earth who are waiting for some additional cosmic shoe to drop."

Henel stared at the man and replied, "The words that you are about to hear have not been told to all. There are but a select few apart from the Godhead that are privy to know what I am about to impart. But El Pneuma hast allowed you access to this tome. You should know that there could be no outcome other than what you have seen. No outcome save the one you have lived. For if God had not allowed the outcome you and many of your kind despise; there would be none to despise it, for creation as you know it would no longer exist."

Henel looked at Argoth his mouth wide open, and he leaned forward to hear more, "But what of choice? What of all the men and women that died in your war. It was Lucifer, was it not who tempted Eve to begin with? I have many readers back home who still think it unfair for God to judge them. What do you say to that?"

Argoth turned his eyes from Henel and stood and walked back to the window and peered outside to see the golden skies of heaven. He sighed then mouthed his reply.

"There were three of us. One is yet present. The other I am told by the Father that I will one day see again. We are the three which assisted in preserving our reality: the three which sacrificed so that El would not turn back creation to nothing. We who attempted to repair the breach to Eternity.

Listen well Henel son of James and understand why your existence is a gift from God. Listen because your question has been posed many times and has taken many forms. But I ask you.

What would you do if you could change the future but in doing so it always led to the same outcome?

What if you were forced to choose between two loved one's eternal destinies? What would you do?

You have asked me, 'What is the nature of choice? Is the future predetermined?'

I was once privy to not know these answers: naïve until the Shattering… before the Breach; before one angel by the name of Lilith sought to obtain vision beyond what he was ordained to see."

Argoth walked from his window to a serving table and poured himself a glass of wine.

He let the drink touch his lips and swirled the goblet and inhaled its aroma.

He returned to take his seat and opened his mouth to speak. "You are a creature that is moved by what he sees. While I could merely explain the Shattering, could explain the possibilities that exist with El, and perhaps quench your thirst for knowledge. I will instead let you witness history in a way none of your kind has ever before seen."

Argoth then walked towards Henel and extended his hand. "Come with me Henel son of James. Come and learn."

Henel stood to his feet and reached to touch Argoth's hand, and when he did they were gone in a flash of light.

Chapter Three

Henel's eyes adjusted to his surroundings, and he noted all about him was white. It was a white that was as encompassing as if a blizzard had cloaked itself in sheets of chalk, and laced in snow.

He lifted his hands to his eyes to protect them from the shimmering glimmer that blinded him and he called out, "Argoth?"

"I am here Adamson. Fear not."

"Where are you?" replied Henel.

"Rescind to the examination of the Chief of Eyes subject: Lilith," said Argoth.

Immediately the room burst into color and flashes of yellows, reds, and blues covered the ceilings, walls, and floors. Henel could barely make out the images, as the walls colors slowed then stopped to reveal a figure of an angel who was seated with his legs and body floating in a lotus position. Images slowly rose from the floor and the walls inched to reveal a diorama of persons and four angels stood before him. Henel's eyes narrowed, and he pointed to the third figure.

"This person here is you. Who are the rest of these men?" asked Henel.

Argoth spoke, "They are my friends; each a spirit of knowledge and wisdom who all vied to lead this great house: Lilith, Raphael, Janus, and of course myself. There were four selected all given honor to lead House Grigori. But only one could be given the God-sight. Only one could become Chief of Eyes. We all had passed our tests. But there was yet still one trial that would eliminate all but one. And it was this test that determined who would be given the God- sight."

Argoth then commanded aloud, "Advance to the testing."

The images changed and Henel watched as all four angels were now seated in the lotus position. Each closed their eyes and immediately clouds lowered themselves to the ground and billowed until nothing but a dense fog hovered over and around the angels. The four angels mouthed silent prayers and white wisps of vapor moved and swirled in eddies. Puffs of living smoke then entered the mouths of all four: each angel inhaled and all opened their eyes and lightning crackled from their pupils.

Then one as the son of man but having wings materialized in front of the four and his person was as a dove yet also that of an eagle and he spoke and when he spoke the words were like waves that crashed upon the shore.

Henel immediately felt the instinct to bow, and Argoth knowing the vision was but a projection nevertheless understood the sentiment and did not dissuade the man to kneel in showing this act of respect. Argoth then decided to support the man's token of worship towards El Pneuma and also kneeled.

"Though four stand before me; only one shall be head. Nebula now searches thee. Who breath of my breath dost thou desire to show my secrets, and to whom will I appoint to lead this great house?"

Henel realized that what he saw was but a recreation and set himself to his feet. He eyed Argoth who also stood and spoke, "When did this take place and what is happening to you?"

Argoth looked on as he watched himself and his peers in the visual display. Janus physically shook and both watched as Janus coughed up puffs of smoke and Nebula emerged from his nostrils and the billowy figure spoke. "This is not the one."

Three now continued unabated and with gritted teeth. All jerked their heads back as El Pneuma looked on stoically, awaiting word from Nebula. Argoth watched as the younger version of himself screamed out in pain.

"ARRRRRGGHHH!"

Immediately a puff of smoke exited from his nostrils and the wavy image of a man could be heard to mouth the words. "This one here... we will watch."

Argoth and Henel watched the remaining two Grigori continue in their spasms, and each turned their heads and their eyes darted back and forth as men who were in a deep REM sleep. They both gazed upwards as if they watched something. Raphael then settled, and a smile stretched across his face and he smiled and spoke aloud. "Mine eyes are thine Lord. Thy will be done."

Lilith also then spoke aloud screaming, "No! NO! NOOO!!!" His head then immediately jerked forward and a billow of smoke exited his nostrils and spoke to El Pneuma. "This one's song is his owns."

Raphael continued to smile, and he laughed. "The sound is sweet my king, and thy sights wondrous to behold. Who am I that I might gaze upon such things and hear of such wondrous things?"

"Nebula?" said El Pneuma.

The wisp of humanoid clouds that were outside of Raphael spoke, "This one sings in psalms and hymns and spiritual songs making melody in his heart. He... he will not release us."

El Pneuma cracked a smile. "He will be a fine leader of his house. Sing with him Nebula and show him what he must see."

Multiple cloud formations then hovered around Raphael and replied as one, "As you croon my king."

Henel stood and he and Argoth watched as his projected image and that of Janus, stared at Raphael, while Lilith continued to cough and the angel let loose the matter of inquiry in his heart. "So Raphael has been chosen?"

The two Grigori nodded.

Janus replied, "It is a good thing. I look forward to seeing what lies ahead."

Argoth mimicked the reply, and as he did, Henel noted that the real Argoth mouthed in unison with his projection and replied. "He is my friend. He will now be our Prince."

Henel watched Argoth closely and while he had seen many an angel display different emotions from time to time he had yet to see any shed a tear as Argoth began to do.

"Argoth?" Henel spoke. "Are you OK?"

The Chief of Eyes wiped a tear from his eye and nodded.

24

"This was when the end began. Here was when the events your people know were set into motion."

Henel looked at him with a puzzled look and replied, "I do not understand?"

Argoth turned from looking at the images and turned to face Henel and replied, "Here, Henel James was reality as you know it, set to change. Here was when a choice was made." He then eyed Henel to return his gaze back to the images. And both Henel and Argoth watched as Nebula was finally released from Raphael's internal croon and Lilith spoke to his newly appointed prince. "With your permission Raphael, I would speak with Nebula and seek an understanding of what I saw."

Raphael nodded. "Permission granted but do not tarry. There is much I must impart, and I have foreseen that you are to watch over the Chief Prince himself: an honor indeed!"

Lilith nodded and smiled. "That is an honor. I will not be long."

Janus, Argoth and Raphael walked from the top of the roof and entered a door that took them below, while Henel and Argoth continued to watch Lilith. Argoth frowned and a scowling look came over him and he spoke. "Here Henel James was eternity shattered."

Lilith then voiced himself to Nebula who still floated in the form of a humanoid fog.

"Great Nebula, I wish to sing a song... I would know the fullness of where the Trance would take me."

"Are you not content Lilith of House Grigori to know the future already given thee? For were you not taken as far as you were willing to see? Be careful to seek more knowledge of that which is to come. Is it not enough to walk by faith and not by sight? Is not the knowledge El hast given thee sufficient? For the future is fraught with many paths. Some lead to El and others... others to a darker place."

Lilith nodded, "I accept the responsibility for that which I will see. I commit to cradle the knowledge given and to be a good steward of its truths."

Nebula floated over Lilith and the living cloud looked above him and stared at him for a moment. "You know not that your future wavers even as we speak. Be not anxious to know more. Press me and I *will* surely show thee. But know that doing so comes with a high price. For you, and yea even all of Heaven."

26

"I have been warned and am clear. Now show me."

Lilith crossed his legs, placing each foot on its opposing thigh. He slowed his breathing and expanded his chest to inhale Heaven's air. Silently he opened his mind to not just see the present but enter the realm of God's allowed possibilities.

The stars slowly faded, followed by the vision of his surroundings into blackness, and all that remained was the movement of galaxies and mirrors of universes reflected back at him.

Deeper he moved into a meditative state and quieted himself in an attempt to attune to the mind of God; to quicken himself to the presence of the Almighty. And commune with He who filled all things, past present and future.

The Shekinah began to emanate over the angel and crackles of electricity arced over him. Slowly Nebula the living cloud lowered over Lilith—singing.

"Who croons the song of the future? Who sings the song of Eternity today?" said Nebula.

Lilith replied, "I am Lilith of house Grigori and stand

27

to accept the mantle of Eye of the Lord. Grant me sight to see the end of all things. Sight to behold what lies ahead."

The white vapor formed a mouth of froth that moved and replied, "Why doth thou seek to know. Is not the knowledge given thee knowledge enough? And with what song do you bring this day that thou may again strum to the hymn of God?"

Lilith prostrated himself to the floor and replied, "I would know the state of things to come. To see what the end may be. If ye deem me worthy, open the fog of the future I pray thee; that if El permits: I might see what lies beyond the shroud that has been called Time."

The cloud then lifted over Argoth and spoke.

"You do not seek to see with the eyes of God. Nay you have asked not for the God-sight but thine own. Nevertheless, El hast approved thy sight, that you might have thy desire so that He may test thee. You are granted sight, but if thou see, you shall be seen in the end for what thou art. Doest thou having been warned still desire this sight?"

"I do," replied Lilith.

The cloud sighed and said, "Then, behold the things that will come."

The living cloud then moved into Lilith's mouth. The color of the angel's eyes changed from yellow to a purplish hue. His body violently jerked back, and he was lifted into the air with his arms extended.

Lilith hovered on his back: he was now a captive in the Trance. His eyes were closed, and they moved as if he was in rem sleep and the Grigori beheld the future: overtaken in the images.

Images of the present flashed before Lilith's eyes, images of his newly assigned charge Lucifer. The Grigori watched as Michael the head of all Kortai swirled in the maelstrom, flailing as he was held fast in the grip of the Abyss as Lucifer summoned a ladder and rescued him from its grasp.

Hazy images swirled from the scene to show a stygian mountain that rose from the depths of Heaven's fertile earth. A mount that belched fire and lava and Lilith watched in horror as the mountain consumed an angel... an Arelim that screamed as it was ingested alive. Once more the clouds of the future became thick and Lilith beheld that Lucifer himself walked through the colon of a great beast of volcanic rock and ash, watched as he summoned a ladder that landed him and a captured angel to the now young earth.

He watched as angels assembled in the gleaming city of Jerusalem and accusations against El flew from the mouths of his angelic brethren over the creation of another species. Indictments of El seeped from murmuring and discontented angelic lips. Lilith watched as Lucifer stood in the midst of the celestial assembly and with fists raised high in anger and with vocalizations that inspired those who listened. He declared that he would ascend to the heights of the clouds and trumpeted he would be like the Most High God.

Lilith's mind tried to assess the images that flashed before his mind's eye and his spirit was overwhelmed with all that he saw. His heart raced, and he began to cough and his body jerked over his unbelieving response to sights that marched in his vision.

Raphael entered back to the rooftop and noted that Lilith was still enveloped in the God-sight: his body convulsed from his in the trance. The newly appointed Chief of Eyes observed the goings on before him and lifted his voice to Nebula who enveloped Lilith in his cumulus grasp.

"Nebula, release him! He cannot take the sight!" yelled Raphael.

Nebula answered as a voice whispers on the wind. "Nay,

prince of God, for the Spirit of the Lord commands it. He will see what he will see and shall not be released before. For his eyes are not satisfied with seeing."

Lilith then let out a blood-curdling scream.

His body began to contort as if a force was twisting his limbs from his body and Raphael reached out to touch him and Argoth who stood by his side grabbed him. "Do it not! Lest you be taken by the cloud to sight unknown. His eyes are his own!"

Raphael lurched from his friend's grip and pointed at Lilith who once more let out a harrowing scream.

"But the Sight... his vision is ripping him apart!"

Lilith heaved and gagged as if he was choking. Nevertheless, Nebula stayed within the angel's lungs consuming the oxygen that Lilith needed to obtain the Sight and remain in the Trance.

Flashing images of war and battles that saw the destruction of the heavenly city assaulted Lilith's mind, pyroclastic stones of fire projected from the Kiln.

Wailing from the skies, Kilnstones rained down upon the host of heaven like hail from a thunderhead. Burning embers screeched dissolution and left smoky contrails as they smashed into all things.

31

And in the vision, Lilith fought with his friend: battling to acquire control of the God-sight. Each engaged in mortal combat with his friend until Lilith saw himself cut down by the hand of the same. Only to see a kilnstone rain down in a fiery tumult and smash atop Raphael consuming the angel within itself, re-compiling his DNA until nothing was left of the angel but a slag of decomposing and smoldering black flesh.

"Noooo!" cried Lilith.

Raphael moved once more to reach for his friend but Nebula spoke from a vaporous mouth that materialized before him. "Do it not! He must see what he chooses, and not before will he be re-leased."

Raphael stayed himself and his face lowered in anguish over the state of his friend.

Lilith continued to watch the images that marched before his eyes. His lungs burned as Nebula withdrew the oxygen from each cell. His fog-like presence igniting the vision that allowed the God-sight. Yet Lilith endured the pain willing to see until his eyes were closed forever, until there was naught in his lungs for Nebula to consume. He would watch until he was but a carcass if need be, but he would finish the sight. He would see what the end would be.

And so he did, as each consecutive vision of the future took its toll, he continued to gaze into the future as his brethren died, gazed until finally, he saw the impossible: Michael and Lucifer at arms with one another, each battling to the death. Fighting until Lucifer repelled Michael's attack sending the angel reeling through the doors of the temple.

Lilith then watched as Lucifer marched himself into the presence of El and raised his sword as the Almighty sat on his throne; watched as he beheld Lucifer's sword draw blood from the heel of God.

Immediately, Lilith's eyes sprang open and his body convulsed, for his heart throbbed within his chest and the angel placed his hands around his neck coughing uncontrollably as he wheezed and attempted to take in gulps of air. Nebula released his hold on the angel's lungs and vacated his body.

"It cannot be!" mouthed Lilith and shaking his head in disbelief.

Lilith plummeted to the ground and his chest rose and fell and he hacked to clear his airway and siphon the life-giving air of Heaven into his lungs.

Raphael placed his arm around him and spoke, "Lilith... are

you OK?"

Lilith stared at Raphael, his face ashen white as he looked into his brother's eyes. He composed himself and slightly nodded, "I… will be fine. I just need to breathe… to think."

Raphael stood back slightly allowing his friend to collect himself. He then placed his hand gently on his shoulder and asked, "What did you see?"

Lilith thought of the images that cascaded through his mind. From Lucifer's rebellion to both his own and Raphael's death, to the bleeding of God; he then turned to face his brother and mouthed a reply.

"The unacceptable."

Lilith then pushed Raphael's hand away and staggered as a drunkard, murmuring one word repeatedly.

"Unacceptable."

Chapter Four

Henel looked at Argoth and asked the angel about what he saw.

"I do not understand. How is this, the beginning of the tale of Lucifer's fall?"

Argoth sighed as the images changed before him, and turned to Henel and replied, "Because here, Henel Son of James; is where deception made its appearance in the realm of Heaven. Here, transparency vanished and duplicity formed in the minds of angels. Here in my house---House Grigori. Although, Talus believes it was the Arelim who incited war: he is wrong. We, the Watchers had knowledge of the schemes of rebellion before rebellion itself reared its ugly head. As it was foretold by David in the book of psalms; even as the Lord made known his ways unto Moses and his acts unto the children of Israel, so to have you only heard and or seen of the acts of Lucifer. You have only observed the results of his desire to upend the Lord and set creation at odds with his creator. Nevertheless, it is we... the Grigori who have witnessed and have understood the deeper truths of his actions: his trafficking, his pride, his desire to steal, kill, and to destroy. We know this human because far before it was ever given life in this realm we had already seen it in Eternity.

We had already fought our war… and won.

Now Henel James, watch and learn the burden that is fore-knowledge."

Argoth pointed to the images that still played on the walls of the Halls of Annals. And Henel set himself to record all that he witnessed.

Raphael had watched as Lilith gingerly made his way into the lower levels of the Hall, and Raphael watched Nebula ascend into the sky. And the angel queried the living breath that permeated the realm of Heaven.

"Nebula, is it permitted with I being Chief of Eyes to see what Lilith saw?"

Nebula rose into the sky. "Aye, Chief of Eyes. But know that thou art summoned to meet with the Godhead."

And in that same moment Argoth had just climbed up the stairwell to the roof of the Hall to relay a message from the throne room. "My prince, you are summoned. It would seem El has already commissioned thy first act as Sephiroth."

Raphael turned from Nebula smiling and spoke out loud, "Of course I am."

He grinned as Nebula wafted away and the living cloud spoke softly as he slowly vaporized into the air.

"See to the business of our king, for you will learn the truth of the vision granted to Lilith soon enough."

Chapter Five

Raphael entered the presence of the living God and bowed as was custom. Surrounding the throne room were his angelic brethren, each sitting in their respective seats at the edge of the throne. Raphael announced his arrival. "My king I stand present as commanded," Raphael noted that El seemed distracted as the Lord did not acknowledge his presence.

"My Lord," said Michael.

"Yes, my son?"

"You seem preoccupied. Is all well?"

El sat on his throne, his eyes looking past them all, looking elsewhere.

"Sasheal has thwarted a threat to Earth, and Apollyon now wonders within himself my actions."

Raphael was stunned at the pronouncement. He looked upon his brethren whose faces also showed confusion, and in amazement Raphael like his peers turned towards their Creator, and spoke. "And your will in this matter Lord?"

El closed his eyes for a moment. He sat in silence, then

opened his eyes, and spoke. "Raphael come forward and report of thy stewardship."

Raphael stepped closer towards the throne and sat. He waved his hands, and volumes of books appeared above their heads and filled the throne room. Raphael stood across from El and pointed to a small window-like opening, and images began to flash before their eyes.

Raphael displayed the record of each Elohim. Each volume was open before him and floated transparently yet occupied no space. Pens and stylus moved of their own accord, never ceasing in their writing. Each pen updated the book upon which it wrote, and in the window before them, Grigori stood everywhere, taking note of all things: watching. Each carried a book, an ink-horn, and a stylus. Each screen showed the cowled and blank face of the Grigori, a race of Elohim that possessed neither eyes nor ears. They could see, but they did not. They heard, but they did not. Gifted with divine sight and hearing, they were absent the instruments normally associated with a species that experiences sight or sound.

El spoke, "Raphael, please display the Grigori assigned to Apollyon's attachment."

Raphael once more raised his hand, and one image came to

the forefront of all others.

The image showed Apollyon looking up, and his Watcher barely perceptible in the background, faithfully recording every word and the thoughts of Apollyon's heart. The Lumazi collectively viewed this crystal display; the show of thought and action hovered above their heads as Apollyon's innermost thoughts were made known for all of them to see.

"El, why didst you not save us?"

Each was amazed; startled even that El would even be questioned.

El spoke, "Lucifer."

Lucifer stood to attend to his master, "My Lord?"

"Please assist Apollyon to understand."

El's eyes fixated upon the person of Lucifer and El began to communicate to Lucifer the words and the voice tone upon which he was to speak the word of God. Nothing was left to chance, and in the seconds that passed between them, Lucifer's reply was straightforward and familiar.

"Yes Lord."

"Thou art dismissed to see to the matter. Make haste," said the Lord.

Lucifer scratched at his chest. "Thy will be done," said Lucifer.

Instantly Lucifer rose to his feet and began his descent from the throne room; deep bass sounds echoed with his every step. Melodious sounds emanated from the motions of his wings, and as he left, the sound of his presence faded.

"Jerahmeel, Talus, and Sariel, I will commence later with your reports. You may each retire for a time, and I will call for you when I am ready. Raphael, I have an assignment for you. Michael, stay: as you also have a new assignment. Gabriel: Sasheal has — fallen. Recover what remains of thy brother's body and bring him here. He has honored me, and I will honor him. Tell your brethren that I am with them and let not their hearts be troubled."

Each cherub bowed before the Lord and then exited the throne room.

El turned to Raphael. "Raphael, thou art commissioned to find all instances of thought, conduct, and or speech similar to Apollyon's. You and your attendants shall bring to me a volume which lists all Elohim and research on your findings."

41

"Aye, Lord. And your desire as to when you would have this complete?"

"Report thou to me on the conclusion of the 6th Earth day at which time I will take my rest."

"As you command Lord," replied Raphael. The mighty cherub bowed then turned to leave the living God.

Chapter Six

Lilith pondered his vision. He turned the images over and over in his mind. Each scene screen burned into his long term memory, tormenting him with the ghost of what he knew was inevitable... his dissolution.

He stumbled from the Hall of Annals and made his way through the hallways of the mountain of God dazed. Passing various members of his kind he wandered dazed through corridors as a drunkard, inebriated by phantoms of truth that plagued his mind like gnats that swirled about one's head.

His angelic peers stared at the Grigori in confusion. But no pleasantries were extended, no courtesy of hello, nothing but the silence and the mumblings of an angel who had seen what none had ever seen... the death of an immortal.

"Unacceptable," Lilith spoke aloud to himself. His mind reeled with the idea that his fate was to die at the hands of he who he called friend, one he competed against for title of Chief of Eyes.

"You will not kill me, Raphael. You will *not* bring deletion! *I* will be deletion. *I* will rewrite this future and expurgate this fate. No, Raphael, *you* will not delete me. *I,* however, *I* will delete you!"

Thought upon thoughts churned over in his mind. Thoughts of how he might escape his prophesied fate. Thoughts how he might reroute the predetermined vision cast. He scurried into a corridor and paced back and forth in thinking out loud on how to undo what the vision had revealed. He stopped and smiled. For El had given all angels choice, and he would use this gift to stretch the limits of what was ordained. He would seek a vision apart from what he had divinely seen and build a future separate from El's. "I will do what none has ever done. I will overturn the future and rewrite it to *my* liking. I will abscond from God himself if need be, and omniscience shall be mine!"

Lilith hurried to the basement of Heaven. An area while not forbidden to angels held a portal to the realm of Aseir and also to the realm of choices Limbo.

Deeper Lilith walked down giant stairs until he entered the dark expanse that was the basement of Heaven. Her pillars carved by the hand of God himself. Her foundation stones laid before Elohim soared the cosmos. For God had made a home and the giant Cadmime beams stretched as bluish girders across the ceilings and floors. Each truss and rafter engraved with the ancient tongue of the Elohim: the language of God.

Lilith approached the back room of the basement until he saw the object of his trek: the swirly mist gate of Limbo.

El had separated the races of Heaven. Seraphim from Ophanim, Elohim from Seraphim; there was once a bridge that crossed a once traversable area of the Maelstrom. But that was eons ago. Before the Schism: before when the Elohim, Seraphim, and Ophanim lived together as one. None has since dared to enter Limbo for it was cordoned off by God. The Gate itself would keep the way and leave one stranded within. So it was said.

Therefore, no one had ever attempted to travel to Aseir. But Lilith was not interested in visiting the land of the Seraphim. He pondered the gate. His desire was to travel among the realm of choices itself. He would not be in violation of the law. He would seek the edges of Limbo to learn the breadth, width, and height of it: to see if other choices brought about differing outcomes. Here he fathomed… here he could explore all options in ad infinitum. Here in Limbo, he could allegedly live out all choices.

Slowly he walked towards the towering stone rimmed gate of glass. Giant square stones formed a curved around it. And within each stone was etched the ancient alphabet of God. One cornerstone was in the script of alpha, and the other to the far right was written omega. As he approached, the mists separated and the polished mirror came more into view. He stared deep into the mirror. It did not seem like a door. The mirror reflected his image: an image that stared at him. Lilith's reflection looked his counterpart over. Eyeing the person that stood before the Gate of Limbo… an image that then smiled, turned, and walked away.

Lilith stood aghast and was startled at what he saw. The image of Lilith turned to look at him as if confused, cocked his head and smiled, and then gestured with a finger for the angel to follow.

Lilith stared at the duplicate. This smiling doppelgänger that beckoned him forward to enter the mirror as it slowly faded from view. He paused for a moment and took several breaths as he considered his actions, exhaled and stepped into the pane of glass.

Slowly the mists swirled once more, covering the angels rear as Lilith now followed Lilith. Grayish white eddies resident within the mirror returned to their churning; their movement masked the angel as he followed his ghostly twin deeper into Limbo's volatile domain.

Chapter Seven

Raphael knew where to begin his investigation... within his own house. The Grigori had access to the combined histories of all things within creation. To review each house would require him to spend much time and go beyond the scope of El's time restraint. To complete his mission, Raphael knew he would have to hurry.

For several of Heaven's hours, Raphael scoured the tomes of his people. Each Grigori was given to one caste. And each caste was tasked to nominate to the Lord one to rule them all. Four representatives of each caste stood for their people: Raphael, Argoth, Janus and Lilith. Raphael thought it made sense to begin with his own house to see if any corruption stemmed from his own people. Looking for anything that was outside the scope of Grigoric law; the angel combed through the works of his people. After several hours of searching, he breathed a sigh of relief as the fidelity of his people's tomes appeared intact.

He sat back in a chair and rubbed his temples realizing that while thorough, this pace was excruciatingly slow and it would take some time to review the whole of all Grigoric tomes let alone those of the other angelic houses.

Perhaps I should focus more on the three heads of each

caste. I could begin with the heads of each house and then work down the hierarchy of the Grigoric order.

With a new plan of attack, Raphael delved deeper into the tomes of his peers, noting each ones particular knack for recording events as required by God yet still retaining their own distinctive voice.

This is much faster. He thought to himself.

Page after page he turned and read the accounts of Janus, but nothing amiss could be found. He moved to Argoth, and no aberration appeared there. Raphael happily breathed a sigh of relief realizing both tomes of Argoth and Janus were free from corruption.

Raphael finally turned himself to investigate the tome of Lilith. All was in order. Every jot and tittle painstakingly kept... until it was not.

"That's odd," Raphael muttered to himself.

He slowly flipped through the tome and the deeper he delved; the more certain he became of his findings: a journal was missing.

No record exists of Lilith's vision with Nebula.

Raphael's eyes narrowed in both curiosity and confusion.

All Grigori's tomes were transparent to no one save the Chief Prince and of course, El. Having been recently appointed by El Pneuma, it was unclear to the angel why no journal entry existed.

Raphael closed his eyes and prayed to his Lord for clarification.

"My king, I have reviewed the records of chief scribe Lilith Grigori. There is no entry depicting the vision-cast he received from thy servant Nebula. Has the scroll been denied me?"

El Pneuma replied in simplicity, "Nay my son."

Raphael rubbed his forehead bewildered. "Then it could only mean that he has not recorded the event. Lord, I request access to this tome."

Instantly, a reply echoed within his heart and mind.

"Seek out Nebula and there he will guide you towards what you seek. For I have told him to expect you, and to grant you vision."

Raphael nodded in acknowledgment and replied in his thoughts, *"Lord, please do not be angry with thy servant, but if you already know what it is I seek, why then do you send me to create this new tome of inquiry?"*

The Lord was silent for a moment then replied. *"The time will come when you will need to make a choice my son. Therefore, it must need be that I reveal to thee the corruption that even now seeps into Creation. Now get thee up for Nebula awaits thee, and soon ye shall know all that need be known. Make hast Raphael, lest my arm be compelled to destroy for the mystery of iniquity doth already fissure into the future."*

Raphael replied, "As you command my king."

Raphael opened his eyes, pushed himself from his desk, and made his way towards the upper level of the Hall. He unlatched the metal clasp that held the roof door in place and opened it to see that Nebula was already awaiting him floating in place.

"We have little time Grigori. We must hurry for there is much to show you, and after you have seen and only then, will you know what must be done. But of more importance, wilt thou consent to do it?"

Raphael walked towards him and as he did he spoke, "I do not know what you mean? Consent to do what?"

Raphael slowly entered the lotus position as was required to concentrate when Nebula entered him.

"Soon, young prince, soon you will see what I see."

Raphael settled to the floor of the roof and with legs crossed, slowed his breathing and queried Nebula, one last time.

"This trance, will it be different?"

Nebula floated before his face and nodded. "Prepare to receive the God-sight young prince."

Raphael then closed his eyes, inhaled through his nose, and then slowly exhaled through his mouth. And when he did, Nebula's gaseous form entered both the nostrils and mouth of the angel.

Raphael breathed in and Nebula filled the whole of the angel's innards. Raphael opened his eyes and when he did his eyes turned white and were ablaze as the brightest star.

Flashes of the past suddenly erupted through his mind.

Exploding bombs of light detonated before the theater of his perception, while image after image paraded before his eyes. From the moment God mouthed, "Let there be light." Raphael saw the burst of galaxies and the brilliant race of the universe gallop to fill the absence of matter that was formerly the Void.

Raphael's eyes quickly moved across his eyelids as he focused his efforts to the actions of his people. He experienced dizziness as the ability to temporarily see all things was overwhelming. Vertigo began to envelop him and he willed his mind to zero in on the actions of Lilith so as not to drift into insanity.

The vision of Lilith who earlier sat on the roof of the Hall, materialized in his mind, and he watched as Lilith had similarly earlier brought his flesh under control that he might receive the flesh of Nebula. Raphael observed as Lilith took in Nebula as he had now done; and watched as the Grigori entered the Trance.

Raphael floated in his mind in a ghost-like form above Lilith and reached out to touch the forehead of his spectral peer.

"Show me Nebula, the sight seen by Lilith. Show me what his stylus has not yet penned."

And within the vision, Nebula reached out and took the apparition of Raphael by the hand, and pulled the angel even deeper into the God-sight. And Raphael beheld a vision within a vision and was allowed to behold all that Lilith had seen.

Raphael watched as Michael and Lucifer sported with one another then observed as the Maelstrom placed them in mortal danger. He viewed the doubt of Apollyon, his journey to murder and the creation of Hell. Raphael's mind reeled as he saw the birth of Charon, and the treason spoken by Lucifer and the rileing of heaven's forces to pummel the land with Ladders. He watched in horror as he and Lilith battled in mortal combat, only to see himself take the life of Lilith to prevent the angels' aid to Lucifer.

Raphael began to hyperventilate.

The vision continued unabated, and Raphael witnessed the destruction of the Kiln. And then his heart beat faster as he watched himself die: run through by a wayward Godstone the result of a battle between his brothers Michael and Lucifer.

His heart rate spiked, and he began to clutch his chest.

"Breathe, young prince," said Nebula. "Calm thyself, and focus: go beyond what you see."

Raphael centered his thoughts on the voice of Nebula and reminded himself that the vision was yet for an appointed time and settled his mind to move beyond the immediate scene of his vision and looked away to follow the trail that continued to lead him onward.

Shaken Raphael shivered and continued to fasten his eyes to the images that raced through his mind's eye. He watched as Lucifer transformed into a deformity of angelic pride and was a three-headed beast with wings that blasted through the temple doors to raise his sword in open rebellion against his father. Raphael watched as his angelic leader lifted his weapon to slice at the heel of God Almighty: making contact so that he actually bled God. The Lord winced, and Raphael watched as the wrath of the Father exiled all those who dared lift themselves in rebellion against Him.

Raphael shook his head in disbelief while his body shivered,; for the visions would not stop, and Nebula knowing what Raphael observed spoke to his mind.

"You now see the rage that is the wrath of Elohim? But despite what thou seest, this is not why El hast brought thee to me. Now see the thoughts and intents of thy brother and when you do, follow the trail of mist that I lay before thee. Do not deviate from the path; neither move ye to the left nor the right; that thou might see what the end of all things will be. For here is where Lilith left the trance. Here he saw that the Almighty allowed himself to be injured; not understanding that the beginning and the end are one with El. Here, Lilith did not understand that it pleased the Lord to be bruised by him; that this act would foretell the efforts of the enemy and display his ultimate defeat. But the pride of life hath taken thy brother, and a rot infests the breast of Lilith. A rot that even now contaminates the Chief Prince... behold."

Nebula then revealed Lilith's thoughts as the angel lifted from the trance and there were thoughts to depose Raphael as the chief prince. Plans and schemes to occupy as Chief of Eye's and to rule by Lucifer's side as Lilith completed the act of dissolution to the Almighty himself.

Raphael was struck; *"He covets my seat?"* he communicated telepathically. *"And does he mean to see these events change; events that will play out to his favor?"*

"Aye," said Nebula.

"But Lucifer's rescuing of Michael hast already transpired. How... how can Lilith bring such a future to pass?"

Nebula was quiet as he exited the nose and mouth of Raphael. Raphael too exited from the Trance, and he noted that Nebula looked away from the angel.

But Raphael noticed his friend's hesitancy and would not be denied his answer. "Nebula answer me!"

The living cloud coalesced into a humanoid form and a frothy mouth began to speak.

"There is but one way great prince; one way that if Lilith desires would shatter eternity as we know it. He must journey into

Limbo and return to a point where the realm of Alpha may be sub-sumed by the realm of Beta, and if successful. Beta would become the Alpha realm."

"Is such a thing even possible?" Raphael replied.

"I am the breath of Heaven. I am that which touches all the lungs of her residence and yea, even beyond. I exist prior to the spark of the Kiln and am brother to the Shekinah, and kin to the Virtues. I speak the truth, Eye of God. There is but one way apart from the Lord himself that reality may be overturned and Limbus my friend; is that way."

Raphael began to understand. He had never entered into the realm of Limbus. It was forbidden. Naught but the Lord traveled the currents of time and Limbus was Time's river. The Lord cautioned that Limbo was the reservoir of Time itself: a realm that emptied into the Maelstrom. He tutored that the place was very much alive and was not the domain of angels. For, it was the living realm of choices: a place where the decisions of all beings lived their alter-nate lives. There, Lilith could explore and mayhap find the choices to create the outcome he desired. There, he could float forever until he found what he wanted... a path to rule the Grigori.

"My apologies, Nebula, follow me please."

Raphael went to the roof door and lowered himself and the living cloud followed. Nebula followed Raphael until they entered the Hall of Annals, and Raphael broke the silence when he spoke to the white walls.

"Location of Lilith Grigori."

Immediately, the room sprang to life and swirls of smoke suddenly showed themselves on the walls of the room. The basement of Heaven could clearly be seen. It was a dark abode and stone ornate columns of onyx mixed with cadmium held aloft God's great house. Angelic runes and symbols adorned the pillars and walls. The room then revealed at the end of the basement of Heaven; a great door of fog. Swirling mists moved within a mirrored gate over 50 cubits high. Obsidian stones etched with the God tongue lined the frame and nothing was behind or within the mirror.

A fog crept from the polished metal and seeped along the earthen floor as a serpent sways. Raphael looked, and the fog formed the shape of a hand that crawled along the ground.

"What is it?" Raphael said as he turned to Nebula.

"It is the Mists, and they are on the move. Lilith hast disturbed the realm. It may already be too late."

Raphael watched as the fog slowly crept its way like an encroaching vine over the obsidian rock of the mirrored gate.

"What is it doing?" the angel asked.

"Exploring this domain and seeking to conform to this realm. If Limbo is emptied of her denizens if the choices locked away do not remain locked; they will consume those within this world; and you, I, and all within *this* dimension will be lost. The Grigori does not understand what he has unleashed... what he has left open to escape."

"Can it be sealed?" Raphael asked.

"Yea, but you must find the fissure to stop its progress; for with every moment we do not, more of the Mists seep into our realm. If they establish a foothold, this reality will be replaced. All shall be awash save El. For the Great One abides in all realms and yet is beyond them. He can never be moved."

Raphael thought hard on the task before him, and the threat that encroached upon this reality. For unbeknownst to Michael and Lucifer, yea even the rest of the Lumazi, Raphael possessed knowledge that would see all that they love overturned. His was to keep the secrets of the Almighty, and before any open rebellion had occurred Raphael was privy that El's children would rebel against him and that many would be cast out. Knew that he himself would be killed in a destructive wake that would result from a coming conflict that Michael and Lucifer would have over who would be God.

Raphael began to understand the depth of the choice that was given to him. A choice to surrender to death so that others might live.

"Nebula, is this realm the best future; the best outcome for my people? If I repair the breach and restore this realm: will it be for naught?"

Nebula's foggy features generated a smile. "Do you trust El angel of God? Did not the Lord say that thou had a choice to thy action? I perceive that those of us who possess the gift of free-will shall always be given the option by the Almighty. He has shared that it is up to thee to do this thing or not. Our fate my friend is in thy hands. For El hath made it so. My trust in the living God is unwavering. Trust in Him as well."

Raphael pondered Nebula's words for a moment and then replied, "I know not my future save destruction by a God-stone. I do however know who holds my present. It is to fulfill the command of the Lord, and He has given me the choice to preserve this realm despite knowing the outcome of my choice. I will exercise… faith. I then choose to trust in the Lord, and though he slay me, yet will I trust him. Go to Nebula and leave me to plan rescue of this realm, for I must prepare and have little time to reverse Lilith's breach of Limbus."

Nebula bowed and lifted himself as a cloud and departed.

Chapter Eight

Henel stood up from his chair and began to pace the room. He looked at Argoth and started to speak then shook his head as if he was conflicted and changed his mind. He then raised a finger and started once more to speak then lowered it and shook his head.

Argoth watched the human as the human paced and eyed him. But Argoth sat still waiting for the question he knew would eventually come, and Henel did not disappoint the angel's expectations.

"You *knew* there was a civil war coming? You *knew* what Lucifer and so many others would do? Your people foresaw all of it. Yet why did you not stop it? Why didn't you intervene? So many of your people... *my* people have died and suffered. And you had advanced knowledge of what would happen. You could have stopped it all."

Henel's eyes narrowed as he peered up and down at Argoth as if he eyed a criminal.

Argoth sat quietly understanding the depth of Henel's statement. Understanding that Mr. James merely echoed from his limited understanding of what he understood of time.

Argoth gazed at Henel and he looked curiously at the man and replied. "You think because I had knowledge of the events preceding them, that I did nothing to prevent the collapse of civilization as I understood it? Is that what you honestly believe Mr. James? Is it your assertion that knowing that trillions would die over our war; that I simply sat idle and left things to *fate*? You do realize that we are in Heaven Mr. James? The very dwelling place of God, and that there is nothing left to chance with El? That He is aware at this very moment, the number of hairs that reside upon your head. He is the Alpha and Omega: the Beginning and the End. Fate is a concept your people have invented due to their willingness to worship the creature more than the creator. No Henel son of James. I moved with much haste to stop the oncoming slaughter that was forthcoming. I did indeed set my hand to the plow to prevent the future and the demise of so many both then and who were yet to come.

But you should know Mr. James, that the future is a finicky thing. I know this because I went into the future and I saw it. I indeed tried to change it. But in doing so I learned a secret: the future cannot be changed. All of our choices exist in the realm of their own living beyond us: the fruit of which always… always leads back to El. And know Mr. James that El has seen *your* future. And He has seen my future, yea even *all* futures. We have only to decide which future *we* will see… which choice *we* will make."

Henel replied, "I do not understand."

Argoth replied, "Of course you do not. The future Mr. James is like the hurricane. It cannot be stopped. It is a force of nature. The scope of its influence cannot fully be grasped until one steps beyond the hurricane or attempts to assess the damage in its wake. Time is likewise. Unable to be fully appreciated until one steps outside of it: to seek to understand the height, width and depth of it. And this is why I have brought you here. To see what others that despite long life have not understood: the wakes and eddies of time. To tell the story as only the Book of Life can tell it. But the question remains Mr. James… are you prepared to hear the rest of the story?"

Henel stood silent for a moment unclear if he should continue. But the journalist in him took over, and he sat down, picked up his notebook and pen and nodded.

Argoth smiled, "Good, then I shall continue, as I most enjoy your company."

Chapter Nine

Lilith followed his doppelgänger and spoke. "Where are you taking me?"

The spirit replied, "Somewhere, where your presence will not invite suspicion. For I know why you are here Lilith Grigori, for I am you and you are I, and I understand as no one else the calling that is in thy heart. And know that I would see your designs succeed."

Lilith stopped as they began to edge away from the basement of Heaven.

"Are we not safe here?"

"No." said Beta Lilith. "We are not, for there are ears in Limbus: ears that are close to the gate and seek to spy the goings on of other realms. I have waited for you; waited since I took the Trance and saw that Lucifer would bleed God. We must move to secure our place, for I refuse to be brought low by the upcoming war between the Chief Prince and Michael."

"Hold, specter of another realm," said Lilith Prime. "How do I know you will help me? How do I know that I can trust you?"

Beta Lilith smiled, "Because I am you. Even now you wonder if your trespass into this realm will give you the advantage that you seek. I know your thoughts and ways as if they were my own. Because of course they are. Alas, you question how you will usurp that which has been lawfully given to Raphael. You have been gifted vision, but you do not possess guile of ruse. For I have foreseen what must be done. And in this realm I have foreseen your coming."

The two floated towards the palace throne room and noted that Lucifer was waiting for El to enter the Kiln. "Step lively twin. When the time is right, I will show you the stone you will abscond. You will take it and with it you will query all of Limbus for eternity if you must. But you will find the option which will most bear fruit and would see us both live and yet also be head of House Grigori. And when you do, you will right all realms so that all exist in unison to one another. For El hath given choice to all creations that are sentient, and I have heard a whisper that He intends to give choice to another yet unmade being. But I have seen that all are not worthy of choice. That to give free-will to so many will cause ruin. Therefore, we must take matters into our own hands. I have seen a vision even further than yours. And we must incite Lucifer to believe that choice should be limited to celestials alone. For a fourth race El will make, and I fear it will dilute the purity that is Elohim and Abomination may well be the result."

"Abomination... I do not understand. What do you mean a fourth race? What are you talking about?"

Lilith Beta sighed, "Know for now that those that are unworthy of choice must serve us. For the younger must serve the elder. Plant this tare into Lucifer's mind and when he is defeated, he will still be a vessel to do our will. A vessel that will assure this fourth race will be a servant and nothing save God himself will be able to rescue them. Do this thing my double, and we will assure that mud and clay will never rise to challenge the stone of the Kilnborn. Do you consent?"

Lilith pondered his doppelgänger's word and replied, "If you show me how to usurp the future... then yea, I consent."

Beta Lilith smiled and replied, "Good, Lucifer enters the Kiln and awaits El. Quickly now, before another grigori sees thee."

Lilith watched as Lucifer and Beta Lilith entered the fiery furnace of life. For here in the confines of the cavern the stuff of life had been deposited, and here God created his race of beings called angels. Stones littered the room, and each sung in harmony. Each made of the disparate elements of creation. Sentient vessels waiting to be fashioned after the Creator's will.

Lilith watched as Lucifer eyed the various stones, watched

as the Chief of Angels surveyed which gem would be given to God, and then would be formed by the same, to ascend to the ranks of the Elohim.

Beta Lilith then looked Lilith in the eye and motioned with his head for Lilith to look to his right. He then spoke aloud that both Lucifer and Lilith could hear.

"The green one there, perhaps?"

Lucifer eyed the gem for a moment then shook his head. "Nay, it is a gem for travel through time and to warp dimensions." There is no Elohim assigned as yet for such a task. I must find another."

Beta Lilith then looked again at his peer and nodded to the gemstone Lucifer had rejected. When Lucifer went deeper into the cavern to select another; Lilith picked up the stone, and it radiated a deep emerald green. Lilith quickly took the gem and placed it in his tome and his tome also began to radiate an iridescent green.

"I am curious," said Lucifer. "It is my understanding that your kind has been commanded to never interfere. I was not aware that Grigori spoke with their charge."

Beta Lilith still unseen to the eye of Lucifer answered aloud that the angel might hear. "Yea, great one: it is indeed not our norm to speak to our charge. But my actions have not interfered with your task. I may indeed choose to speak to a charge if I so choose."

Lucifer harrumphed, "Interesting, that you would seek to speak now. I have walked up and down the midst of the stones of fire since the beginning and have never had another save El ever speak to me within the cavern. I am curious grigori… what has changed?"

Beta Lilith was silent. He knew that Lucifer was extremely cunning and chose his response carefully.

"The chamber is appropriate. For there are none that can hear our conversation save you. I may converse with thee and yet still keep the charge assigned. Carry on Chief Prince for I must note your words and actions. And I do not wish to contaminate my journaling with unnecessary prolonged conversation. Please proceed with your selection."

Lilith understood that Beta Lilith bought him time to vacate the Kiln before El had arrived and quickly dashed out the room. He scurried himself to the basement of the palace making sure to not be seen lest he draw suspicion from the Grigori who might wonder why the Lilith of this dimension was not with Lucifer. He then walked the dim steps back towards the Gate of Limbo and stood before it.

His glowing greenish tome now imbued with the Godstone in hand.

"Let me see the creation of the fourth race."

The misty gate swirled and a green jade glow enveloped the frame of the mirror and the gate illuminated showing a beautiful garden in the foreground. Lilith confidently walked through to see what his counterpart referenced.

To see this new creature of mud and clay that would also be given the gift of choice.

And unbeknownst to the angel, a small chip revealed itself in the mirrored doorway, and crept across the ancient gate.

Chapter Ten

Raphael called Janus and Argoth into his chambers and had both angels sit down. He looked at them quietly; each one stared back at him, waiting for him to speak.

Janus broke the silence and spoke. "Raphael, I have never seen you so troubled. If something vexes you, then speak my friend."

"Agreed," said Argoth.

Raphael nodded and replied. "I have just come into my station as head of this great house. And already I am tasked with duty from El to determine the source of thought corruption that has seeped into the realm."

Argoth looked at Raphael not understanding, "What do you mean *thought corruption?*"

Raphael then opened his chest and pulled out the beating tome within him and played back for the two the thoughts of Apollyon. An angel who had questioned God's goodness whilst he watched another angel stop a solar flare from destroying the newly created world El had made. Each angel observed as an angel by the name of

Sasheal had raced to intercept and interject himself into the path of a solar flare that emanated from Sol and sprinted towards the Earth: a flare that was the result of Apollyon's lack of concentration in his control of the star. Together the trio watched as Sasheal became flesh that he might interact with the flare and all watched as he absorbed the star's energy and fell to the earth. But it was the recorded words of Apollyon that caused both Argoth and Janus to gasp. *"El why didst you not save us?"*

Both angels watched as El then turned to Raphael and spoke. "Raphael, thou art commissioned to find all instances of thought, conduct, and or speech similar to Apollyon's. You and your attendants shall bring to me a volume which lists all Elohim and research on your findings."

"Aye, Lord. And your desire as to when you would have this complete?"

"Report thou to me on the conclusion of the 6th Earth day at which time I will take my rest."

Raphael then ceased his tomes display for the duo and reached to place the book back into his chest.

Raphael looked at the faces of his friends and spoke. "Speak what is in thy heart."

Argoth was first to reply. "It is unthinkable that an angel would question the actions of God? Who is this angel that he would suppose on El so?"

Janus also released his mind on the matter. "Apollyon has witnessed something that I think would make anyone of us wonder why El did not simply bring the solar flare to a halt. But to conjecture the mind of the Almighty is foolishness. For his ways are not our ways, nor his thoughts our thoughts, and his ways are past finding out. One would have a greater chance to speculate the depth of the bottomless pit than to understand all that moves the Almighty. What we do know is what has been revealed. El allows us free-will: allows us choice to act. We are not as the beasts he has made. But, if El's goodness is questioned and is not established..."

Janus paused to ruminate more before he continued. "Reality as we know it will be questioned. For El's goodness is the foundation by which we exist. If others begin to believe in goodness apart from El... their own perhaps... it could alter reality as we know it."

Raphael nodded, "Agreed. Thus, I have begun my search per El's instructions and believe I have determined that another source exhibits the same corruption."

Argoth suddenly scanned the room and looked to his left and

72

right and spoke. "Where is Lilith; should he not be here to deliberate? Was he not also chosen to lead as head of Grigori?"

Raphael let out a sigh and replied, "Lilith is the source of the corruption that has questioned the goodness of God. Even now unbeknownst to all save we in this room. He has moved to undermine the will of the Almighty: to… disobey."

Janus and Argoth both looked at Raphael in disbelief. "How is such a thing possible? This cannot be!"

"It is as I say," said Raphael. "I have communed with Nebula and have entered the Trance. I have seen with the God-sight and watched as Lilith has left this realm and has entered the forbidden realm of Limbo. He is not *here*."

"Limbo?" replied Argoth. "For what purpose would he journey there? Has not El stated it off-limits?"

Janus nodded in understanding. "Limbo is the realm of choices, the reservoir of choices unmade, and the alternative of decisions not taken. It is the realm of alternate realities. Did Lilith see something he seeks to change? A decision or outcome he wishes to undo?"

Raphael nodded his head. "I believe so."

Janus then looked at his friend and his narrowed, "You have not told us what the God-sight has revealed."

Raphael breathed in deeply, looked away and then replied. "I have not."

Janus sighed and his face developed a sad smile, "It would seem my friend that the burden of Chief Prince is indeed heavy. Very well then, I will not press you on the matter."

"Agreed," said Argoth. "You have called us here to inform us and inform us you have. But what is it that you require?"

"I have not informed you of all," said Raphael. "For Lilith's departure into the realm of Limbus has brought with it a fracture within the barrier that separates Limbus from our own. Even as we speak, the mists of Eternity seep through into our realm. This breach must be sealed. I cannot do it alone and I need you to assist me in the rifts closure."

Argoth looked at Janus and they both nodded, "We are at your service. Go on."

"Lilith is the reason the breach exists. His presence in the realm merely keeps the passage open. He must be brought back to the prime reality in order to seal it for good. I cannot go for someone must stay behind to attend to the breach and the mists possible incursion. Nor can I leave my post as Chief of Eyes to return him. I need you two to do this for me, our house and for the realm."

"And if he chooses to stay despite command to return," said Janus. "What then?"

Raphael's face grew stern. "I have contemplated this and I fear he will *not* comply as his actions have clearly placed him outside the authority of El. He is considered rogue and any and all notes from his pen and tome are to be redacted. His letters cannot be allowed to contaminate the Book of Life. Bring him back alive if possible, but if not..." Raphael's voice trailed off in sorrow.

Argoth frowned and nodded, "Understood. We will do what must be done."

Raphael continued, "Know that Lilith's presence within Limbo places the whole of creation at risk. The longer he remains in the domain, the longer the mists may seep into our own and transform this realm. If enough of the void-clouds enter... they will reshape our reality and possibly even turn it back to a state prior to God voicing, "Let there be light." We cannot allow this to happen. You, therefore, will be my Redactors. It will be your purpose to scour his tome and to erase changes to the realities that you encounter; including the erasure of our brother himself if necessary. Will you help me?"

"Of course," said Argoth. "Will we be using the assist of the other houses?"

Raphael shook his head. "This is an issue for the Grigori. He is one of us. If the situation grows beyond the means of our house to contain, then I will summon the council and submit to the wishes of the Chief Prince on the matter. Until then my concerns are conjecture wrapped in layers of possibility. Such is the way of Limbo, and none are better equipped than House Grigori to solve this dilemma. For now: I shall wait."

Both angels stood to their feet and bowed to their friend and elected Prince over house Grigori. "We are thine to command. We will let none of the words of El fall to the ground."

Raphael also stood to his feet and nodded. He proceeded towards the two and placed his hands on their strong shoulders.

"Both of you... kneel. And I will make of you a new caste of Grigori. Thou shalt be my Redactors."

Both angels kneeled as commanded and Raphael laid his hands atop their heads and spoke a pronouncement over them.

"Thou art now voice of my voice, and jot to my tittle. To write or rewrite as the pen of God, I now grant thee. To move through the ether and to enact the judgment of God and of house Grigori against those that are out of the way I command thee. A new ledger I now give and a page from the Chief of Eyes: a page to track down those who comment or edit contrary to the rule of Grigoric law. Go forth my Shaun-tea'll and correct the tomes that thou find." Raphael then took his tome from his own breast and from it tore two unwritten pages from the book and took his hands and clutched at the tomes within the chest of each angel before him and inserted a page from his own into theirs.

"From the journal of the Chief of Eyes I now tear. You are my extension as my power now flows through you. Represent our house, the Lumazi and the Lord thy God well. Rise Redactors. Rise my Shaun-tea'll."

Both angels then took the new ledgers changed by the insertion of their leaders' own page and reinserted the books into their chest cavity beneath their robes. Power flowed through them both as never before and their bodies shimmered, and each stood to their feet.

"You have been entrusted with virtue," said Raphael. "Be

thou a good steward; you will be able to track Lilith through the realms. Now let us go for he must hurry for if we delay, a night shall come that no one may work."

He turned to exit the room and his two comrades followed their leader as the three left Raphael's suite and traveled to the underskirts of Heaven to the gate of Limbo.

* * *

Raphael, Janus and Argoth made their way to the basement of Heaven and stood next to the portal to Limbus. Fog crawled from its mirror-like opening and slithered across the floor. Raphael frowned as he looked upon the dread mist and spoke. "I will need to stay behind and contend with the mist. It is not yet of a substance where it can contour to our surroundings. It cannot be allowed to coalesce and consume this realm."

He then reached into his robe and revealed his tome for his brethren to see. He turned to a blank page within the journal and ripped two pages from the volume, folded it and gave one folded piece of paper each to Janus and Argoth.

"Here, take these pages, they will allow me to track you

through the realms of Limbo. As long as you hold it in your possession I have means to bring you home. Lose this: and the way will be lost to me. Beware, for if such occurs you could be stranded in a reality that while similar is yet foreign to all that you know. Remember, find Lilith. I have conjectured that he has taken a Godstone and forged it to manipulate either reality or time, perhaps both. You must find both he and the stone or all is lost. If he will not submit to return… then you are authorized to redact our brother and bring his tome to me by any means necessary. Am I clear?"

Both Janus and Argoth replied, "We are clear."

"Then go," said Raphael, "And may the Lord God go with you."

Raphael then closed his eyes and the mirror of mists shimmered and within its reflections varied locales of Heaven appeared for a moment, and then disappeared to show another. Raphael watched as differing scenes misted into view and spoke, "Both of you… on my mark jump into the mists and you should arrive at your correct destination."

Another locale changed.

"Make ready!" said Raphael.

79

The locale then changed and the mirror then showed the three angels in the basement of Heaven. It's visage merely replicating their presence.

"Now!" Raphael roared.

A jade hue suddenly and unexpectedly shimmered over the mirror and a fracture materialized and slowly inched across the seeing-glass.

Raphael's eyes grew wide and his face turned ashen white and he screamed out in a shrill voice for the two to halt... but it was too late.

Both Janus and Argoth had leaped into the mirror and their momentum carried them through the doorway into Limbus.

Chapter Eleven

Janus walked through the mirrored gate of Limbo and he immediately felt himself become dizzy. Grayish fog swirled around him and distant voices whispered in his ears; calls from the ether that serenaded to him to follow their voice. To choose this over that and to embark to the right or to the left of the glowing path that was laid before him. He was on solid ground this he knew. But the darkness about him was a black surrounded in ebony. Janus strained with his eyes to see beyond the trail that he walked and whenever he thought to venture even in his imagination from the path set before him he began to shiver uncontrollably.

He steeled himself and continued to follow the lit pathway. He intuitively felt the need to quicken his pace. To escape that gnawing that he must hurry lest he trapped in the darkness of whispering entities that called to him, for as the whispers increased in their call, he sensed something reach to him from the darkness: a hand. A hand that attempted to pull him into the dark and away from the lighted lane that stretched before him.

Again something touched his arm.

Startled, Janus looked but saw nothing and began to sprint down the path towards an approaching light that raced to meet him in the distance.

The whispers now grew more directive and louder.

"This way," said a voice.

"No, over here," beckoned another.

"Come, feed us. Feed the Mists."

Janus ran as ghostly apparitions began to appear to his left and right; smoky figures that moved with him, floating as flickering clouds over water; each weaving towards him and then swinging back into the blackness.

"We are the in-between of the tick and the tock: the personified glimmers of choices not taken, will you not abide in the infinite loop of mirrors? Why make haste to leave immortal. Stay… stay and feed the Mists."

Janus focused on the path before him and as ghostly hands reached out for him he pushed and shoved his way through phantoms of choices that began to materialize and form into solid beings before him.

Humanoid shades of his choices past.

The choice to lead his caste: the choice to leave the

Trance and submit to the rule of his other brothers. Choices that became more tangible as he pressed towards the light of his objective.

He exited the portal of Limbus, the tunnel which he traveled and when he did gaunt hands flailed and attempted to grapple him to pull him from escaping the foggy domain of election.

"We are ever here... your choices that you have left behind. We are ever waiting... waiting to take flesh."

Janus broke through the barrier of light and when he did he found himself within the throne room of God. Stumbling, he situated himself near a pillar towards the rear of the room and listened quietly as El began to speak.

"In this day I shall take my rest," said El.

"In this day you will have great tribulation, but be of good cheer. I have placed my faith in you. Rest your faith in me, and you shall come forth as pure gold," said El.

Michael and the rest of the council knelt before their God and listened to their Lord. El smiled and looked down upon them.

"My children, I leave you but for one day that all should be accomplished in accordance with my will." El then closed his eyes.

Immediately, the Shekinah Glory grew dim, lifted from off El, and rocketed out the palace flying over the city and towards the edge of Heaven, then dissipated to parts unknown. The light of Heaven retreated as the setting of the sun. The mountain of God grew dim and darkness crept over all the land. As the host of Heaven looked upon the dimming sky, a fog rose from the ground. The temperature dropped and all of Heaven felt El's immediate presence no more.

Janus then felt his body adjust to the chill in the air. His awareness of El was distant almost non-existent. It was a sensation of blindness that left him dizzy and he collapsed to his knees. A sound of a hammer hitting metal then came from the side of the chamber of the Kiln and as the Lumazi scurried to investigate; Raphael saw movement from the corner of his eye and saw his friend collapse to the floor.

"Excuse me for a moment. I must attend to another matter."

Michael nodded as the rest of those assembled went

to investigate a protruding bulge they noted in the Kiln's door.

Raphael caught Janus by his shoulders as the struggling angel looked at him smiling. Raphael tilted his head as he paused to examine the angel that he held aloft.

"You are not *my* Janus. Who are you?"

Janus mouthed but one word… "Danger…" then collapsed into his friend's arms.

* * *

Lilith had explored the realm of Beta, one of the known dimensions of existence. His moving forward in time within the realm showed him that a fourth race was indeed coming. So the angel continued his travel through multiple dimensions until he settled upon the realm of Theta. His observations noted that in each realm there were two personalities upon which all divergent paths branched: Lucifer and Michael. Lilith thus devised a plan to influence the Chief Prince Michael to stop the downfall of Lucifer before the angel's actions could bring about the collapse of a third of Heaven; a demise that he had foreseen was assured to occur in his own realm.

85

Perhaps in this realm my dissolution could be prevented, he thought.

Therefore, the angel committed to spy upon Michael of the Kortai and followed him to the angelic meeting of assembly and kept himself unseen from the eyes of his invisible brethren. Hidden from the Grigori Lilith waited whilst the heads of angelic houses discussed matters of state. And after a time when Lucifer departed to go planet-side and Raphael was attending to the task given to him by El. Lilith found a moment after the Lumazi dismissed where he could be alone with the head of the Kortai.

Lilith waited until all the other angels had left and then inconspicuously entered the council chambers. Michael still stood at the head of the table and re-rolled scrolls from his meeting and began to deposit them back on the shelves that lined the room.

Lilith appeared but an arm's length from the angel and spoke. "Hail Prince of the Kortai, may I have a word?"

Michael turned startled for the voice the invisible voice for he did not see the angel enter the chamber and replied. "You are a Grigori. Why doth a Watcher seek my attention when not even my own appears?"

Lilith was able to see Athamas the Grigori assigned to Michael and nodded. The angel invisible to Michael returned Lilith's salute and spoke. "My duke, I did not expect your arrival. Do you wish to relieve me of my post at this time?"

"Nay, replied Lilith. Stay, hear and record as is our way. What I say is for not just the Prince but for thee as well. You may reveal thyself so as not to make the prince uncomfortable."

Athamas then uncloaked and Michael saw that both Grigori floated in the room, and Athamas was floating only feet away from him his stylus journaling the encounter.

Lilith spoke, "I trust that you are satisfied Michael. This is Athamas of my caste. What I have to say is for his ears as well."

Michael sat and looked at the two angels curiously. "Why do I not receive report from thy liege?"

Lilith floated towards Michael closer and replied, "Because I fear that the corruption that my master looks for has infected the Lumazi, and I have come for the sake of Heaven to one outside my house. And I fear that my own house has fallen to the mystery of iniquity."

Michael's eyes lit up curiously. "Say on."

"I am Lilith of House Grigori. This one here is Athamas, but

I am not Lilith of this realm. For I have crossed the gates of Limbus to deliver a message to thee. A message of impending doom that if not stopped will encompass the whole of heaven and nay creation itself. A doom my prince, of the soon coming clouds of war."

Michael's neck drew back in disbelief. "War... what is this war you speak of? And why are you in this realm and not thine own?"

"Because my prince, for my realm, it is too late. For by the time you hear the entirety of my words; my dimension will have taken the path of conflict; a conflict to unseat El."

Athamas couldn't help but gasp, and Michael himself was wide eyed and his jaw was open. "I hold your words suspect. How do I know that what thou say to me is true?"

"Because my prince this one here knows that only a few of my kind are given the God-sight; sight to see the future and to know those things that shall be. I am one of those in my house. Now I am come to make thee understand what shall befall thy people in this day: for yet the vision is even upon us now. But know that even whilst you are here. There are some in this land that seethe with pride to obtain a station that can never be. Your land will see war at the hands of Lucifer. He will march upon the temple and yea even bleed God. But know that God has ordained that this should be. To give space for the flowering of all his children's desires that he might know the heart of them. And even now Raphael knows that this knowledge must separate thee from he. For the vision is even nigh thee and it shall speak and not lie: it will not tarry. So behold prince of Kortai and see what I have crossed dimensions to show thee."

Lilith then reached into his chest and withdrew his tome. The beating heart of every Grigori and lifted it for Michael to see. He then ripped a page from it and threw it into the air. Immediately images filled the room and ceiling and Michael and Athamas watched as Lilith played for them the imaginings from his Trance. Each angel watched as Lucifer entered Hell, rescued Abaddon. They watched as Talus and Gabriel fought one another and Michael entered the Kiln to create the sword of Ophanim; watched as Lucifer and he battled for supremacy to keep the chief prince from entering the temple. Michael watched only to see himself fail as Lucifer raised his sword to smite God's heel and draw blood.

The vision then stopped and Lilith spoke. "Know that after God is bled, the great one will arise and Heaven will be torn asunder and the kiln destroyed; a destruction that you will cause in your battle with Lucifer. Know my prince that Lucifer will with a third of

89

heaven rend the earth and bring El's newborn children, the humans to heel, and they will be subject to death and one day even rise to destroy Yeshua. Know this my prince that the vision is sure, and I have seen it. I come to stop the corruption that now spreads throughout the realm. A standard allowed by El to roam the dimensions and to raise alarm that ye might not perish in His wrath. I come my prince, because only you can stop Lucifer; of this I have also seen. And the Raphael from my realm will rage over my revealing the secrets of the Sephiroth, and will surely follow me and will lift up his hand against me. Thus I seek asylum under the banner of house Kortai and leave myself to your judgment."

Michael and Athamas both looked at Lilith with incredulous stares and were both in shock.

Athamas in particular shook his head and voiced denial. "How can this be possible?" He spoke.

Michael was quiet then stood to his feet and walked towards this courier of incredible news. "Athamas, do you believe him?" Michael asked as he eyed Lilith up and down weighing what he had heard.

Athamas replied, "He is head of my caste, one selected to lead the house of Grigori. He has torn the thing from his journal.

How can it not be otherwise?"

Michael nodded, "So be it. You will have my protection. But you did not just come this way to give warning. What would you have me do?"

Lilith frowned, "There is but one thing that can withstand the power that will soon be wielded by thy brother if he is not stopped. You must forge the Sword of Ophanim and you must stop your brother before it is too late."

Michael scrunched his face in uncertainty. "Sword... stop him how?"

Lilith frowned and replied, "Dissolution my prince. Lucifer must be killed before he can ascend to power and destroy us all."

* * *

Lilith after his discussion with Michael set upon himself to speak privately with Argoth and Janus of Theta realm. Argoth paced back and forth as both he and Janus weighed the words of Lilith Prime.

"What you are asking us to do is to commit betrayal to our

house; to hide your intentions from our High Prince. You realize this do you not?"

Lilith looked squarely are Argoth and replied. "You have seen the vision cast. It does not lie. There is war coming upon you whether you desire it to be so or not. You must choose if the honor of Heaven is more to be obliged than the honor of our house. For what is greater, the house, or he that builds the house? And are not all our houses but the work of El's hands?"

Janus then spoke, "But should we not give Raphael the opportunity to answer and give decision?"

Lilith shook his head. "Raphael is going to die Janus; destroyed by a rain of fire due to the Kiln's destruction. He knows this already and has yet to speak of it. He has already decided to allow the events he has seen to play out. Otherwise *he* would intervene. But is the law of non-interference not made to service us? Or *we* made to service the law?" Lilith raised his hands in frustration. "Raphael has made his choice. Lucifer is going to come for him. We can stop him now before it rages to the point where billions will be lost... billions cast from Heaven. Will you not lift a finger to save a third of our kind? For if not, what is the use of mere documentary as we watch our brethren, nay Creation itself pass into oblivion?"

Lilith then walked towards the two angels and placed his hands on their shoulders. "Do what you think you must. But I will protect Raphael with my life, even from himself…" He paused and looked each angel deep within his eyes and continued. "…even if it means the death of the Chief Prince."

Lilith then turned to walk away and said. "My peer even now knows the change taking place within the Chief Prince's heart. But he is bound to keep what he knows to himself. Soon Lucifer will go planet-side and assist in the organization of the globe's angelic hierarchy. He will watch as El makes a garden for the fourth race; our soon coming siblings. We must preemptively smite him before he arrives back to Heaven from this task. For once he does the vision will begin to come to pass. So are you with me? Or will you stand and let Raphael and billions of Heaven's people die?"

Janus sighed and followed Lilith looking at Argoth as he did.

Argoth inhaled then echoed Janus in his groan and wondered within himself if Heaven was already torn asunder.

"I am coming," he said.

Chapter Twelve

Argoth Prime walked through the looking glass and immediately darkness was all about him. He could hear whispers in the
dark but only for a moment, for as fast as his eyes were surrounded
by black he squinted for the brightness of the light that now beamed
over him. He raised his hands to shield his eyes and stepped into
the gleaming brilliance of the shining door before him; a door that
deposited him into the realm of Theta.

His eyes adjusted to the view, his pupils slowly came into
focus and what he saw astonished him.

Raphael was fending off Michael the High Prince with a
dagger flying around his person. Sparks of light from metal impact-
ing against metal lit the atmosphere and Raphael was backpedaling
in a desperate attempt to keep his distance from Michael. Raphael
opened portal after portal to delay Michael's aggresive march towards him. He then opened a portal into the realm of space, and
stars and galaxies suddenly appeared behind Michael. He turned
when Raphael opened a portal once more and Michael was sucked
away and in the blink of an eye was gone.

Raphael breathed heavily, and he nervously looked behind
him. Argoth followed his eyes to see what he protected and uncon-

scious on the ground mere feet away was Lucifer coughing up blood. Raphael ran to him and looked at a wound the angel had sustained to his chest. Blood oozed from it and Lucifer's body was bruised and battered as if he had been in a physical confrontation and had lost.

"I cannot hold him off forever, my prince." Raphael said as he knelt down towards him. "He is momentarily beset by the power of a galaxy's gravity well. But it is only a matter of time before he returns. I can only forestall him but not stop him."

Lucifer nodded in understanding and replied, "I do not have the power to summon a ladder. Michael will not be the only one to seek my life."

Argoth immediately ran to their side and revealed himself. "What has happened? Why are you fighting with Prince Michael?"

Lucifer then looked up startled as he eyed the uncovered angel that now stood near them.

Raphael looked at Argoth and his dagger flashed into view and it flew towards him until it straightway was poised at Argoth's throat.

"You are not Argoth… at least not *our* Argoth. Are you the reason for the carnage Michael has unleashed upon Heaven? Lilith,

95

protect the Chief Prince!"

Immediately Lilith-theta, Lucifer's Grigori in this realm materialized, and he too stood over the Light-bringer and his pen turned into a dagger and both Grigori stood ready to defend Lucifer at all costs.

"I asked you a question impostor! I will not ask again. Why are you here and are you for us or for our adversaries?"

Argoth weighed his words carefully and knew that the Lilith in front of him was not the angel he was searching for. He lifted his hands up and his palms outward in a gesture of surrender and spoke. "You are right my prince I am not of this realm, but from what I call the Prime realm or Alpha. I have come to apprehend the renegade Lilith who hath defied our order and has breached Limbo. I know this one here is not whom I seek. Be still and know that within my breast beats a new tome that has been bolstered by the Raphael of my time. Allow me to show thee, that I may grant help if at all possible to your cause."

Raphael replied, "Show me, and be quick about it."

Argoth nodded and reached gingerly within his breast to reveal the tome. Its pages were gilded and Raphael noted that on its edge were pages that matched those from his own tome. The blade at Argoth's throat lowered, and it returned to the form of a stylus.

"I see my fingerprints within your volume. You have been entrusted indeed Redactor. I will grant you the courtesy as one that I have appointed to such a task should have. You have shown thyself to be honor bound to me in your realm. Correct?"

Argoth nodded, "The thing is as you say."

"Then you will take the Chief Prince and Lilith to the place I shall send you and there you will protect Lucifer from all foes. Are you clear in your purpose?"

Argoth bowed, "I am clear my prince."

Raphael-theta then began to open a portal and Argoth lifted the prince of angels and took Lucifer into his arms.

Lightning suddenly materialized behind Raphael and the ground shook and an explosion of light filled the area.

Thunder immediately followed and Michael was ablaze in white light; holding the Sword of Ophanim facing Raphael. The angel's face was grim, determined,… and angry.

He then ran its blade through Raphael and catching the prince of Grigori off guard.

Raphael let out a scream, and he grabbed the handle of the sword which pierced his body and looked at Michael.

"Brother…" he said. Raphael then turned his head and spoke with his dying breath to Argoth and Lilith, "Quickly! Off with you now!"

Lilith flew into the portal as Michael's face grimaced in rage and anger and the sword that held Raphael then split into seven swords exploding Raphael's body into chunks of angelic flesh.

"Raphael!" Lucifer screamed in horror, attempting with all his might to be released from Argoth's grip and strike at Michael. But Argoth's hold was sure and Lucifer was in a weakened state and Argoth ran with the struggling angel and jumped through the portal as it began to collapse.

Michael, stymied by his inability to follow, and his killing of his brother; fell to his knees and rocked back and forth over what he had done. He stared at the blood of his brother upon his palms and released a guttural roar of anguish; his hands clenched into fists as he pounded the ground and wept.

* * *

Raphael watched as his comrades jumped into the doorway to Limbus. He noted the jade hue that unexpectedly shimmered over the mirrored door and the ensuing fracture that materialized and clawed across the seeing-glass of mist. But it was too late to recall his friends. Too late to know if they were lost in the eddies of Limbo or if they had been transported to their appropriate destination. He could only wait… and pray.

Raphael examined the fissure. It was much larger and wider now. And it was only a matter of time until it spread, and unleashed the pent up Mists of decisions that multiplied within all dimensions and coalesced within the realm of choices. For now there were three denizens who were outside of their domains roaming within Limbo: each one's presence now exerting a pressure on the misty gate; causing it to expand and fracture the runes and seals that El had built to contain alternate realities.

Ancient seals designed to prevent a cascade breach into the Prime realm: the Alpha realm. For, Limbo was the storehouse of all choices and the reservoir of decisions not made. Through this realm one could know the extent and the capability of one's actions. In this causeway to other realities, one could judge the multitudes of all choices.

Omniscience was not a thing to be sought after; nor a trifle bauble to seek. Only El could absorb all possibilities... could *see* all futures. Even as the Sephiroth, Raphael was limited to see but one generation ahead. He could not see all outcomes and the myriad of forks each would create ad infinitum.

Even he could not see like El.

Raphael stood before the swirling gate and held no desire to see released the totality of all choices that God would allow.

A cracking was heard and then the sound of hissing exploded above him.

The pressure in the room suddenly dropped and a greenish fog seeped into the chamber from a larger fracture and bled into the room.

Raphael knew he must act quickly.

Getting dizzy the angel pulled from his chest his tome and raised his hand. Power flowed through him. Power as the Sephiroth, for Raphael's was to know what God allowed. And the angel's knowledge was vast indeed. He moved his hands and circles of power appeared before him and his tome emblazoned in white light and he took a page from the rear of his journal and flew over the opening to cover the breach, and the journal's page held fast. The sound was as if a vacuum had been sealed and the pressure of the room slowly returned to normal. The angel yawned to make his ears pop, and he shook his head. He could feel a warmth slowly seep down his face. Raphael wiped his nose, and blue blood that coursed through his kilnstone stained his hand.

He eyed the gate, scanning for any additional fissures and or cracks that might expand. Limbo was the road to the city of Aseir: the home of the Seraphim. If God did not make allowance to cross the way safely, passage was impossible. And Raphael was very much aware of what lied behind the mirror; knew because his own reflection appeared and stared back at him smiling... smirking.

He watched as his own likeness eyed the gates contours and reached its hands up as if to inspect the cracks that fissured across the glass and gas-like doorway from its side of the portal. The ghost then viewed Raphael's makeshift bandage and stared at it and grinned.

The creature then lowered its eyes to gaze into Raphael's own and then tilted its head in a gesture of amusement: shaking its head at the angel as it turned to walk away into the gray ether and

101

the black cloak of swirling darkness.

Raphael watched the smoky apparition depart and stood defiant like a sentry guarding his post. He too then raised his eyes to view his work in preventing the beings release, and inhaled as he noted small fissures slowly continuing their snail's pace and unabated march. He then exhaled and muttered under his breath.

"Hurry my friends… please hurry."

Chapter Thirteen

Janus awoke to the smell of Mirabel honey and his eyes focused that he was in a bright chamber and attempted to rise only to find that his wrists and ankles were bound to a stone table.

He struggled against his straps and attempted to mist through but was unable.

"I have removed thy tome from your breast," said Raphael Chi. "I have taken the time while you were asleep to read your chronicle. It appears that you are not of this realm and my counterpart in the Alpha realm; hast imbued you with power beyond that of your peers. I have read your story Janus. But I would hear the rest of the matter from thine own lips."

Janus lifted his head and gestured to the manacles that held him. "Are these necessary? If you have indeed read my tome then you should know why I am come."

Raphael Chi walked towards his Grigoric peer and looked down upon him. "I know why you came through Limbus yes, but why are you *here*?"

Raphael waved his hand and the manacles which held Janus

flew open.

The angel raised himself to sit on the stone slab and rubbed his wrists. A cup of Mirabel tea floated towards him.

"Drink," Raphael said. "It will help restore your strength. There is manna leaf as well should you desire it."

"Thank you," said Janus. "I would like some very much." Janus reached for the leaves and dipped them into the sauce his people made to accompany them when eating.

"I am here to apprehend and extradite Lilith back to the Prime realm."

Raphael sighed, "I am afraid that you will find that challenging to do; for he hast already gone to the brothers Lucifer and Michael and convinced them that I have betrayed El. He has given them foresight into the creation of the fourth race."

Janus's eyes brows drew together, and he quickly swallowed his food, looked at Raphael and replied. "How do you know this?"

Raphael motioned with his hands and a wall illuminated and displayed that a large armed entourage approached the Hall of Annals with spears and swords. An entourage led by the brothers and Lilith and his twin floated behind them with other Grigori in tow.

"The Hall grants me sight of all things. I have been judged a traitor by the Lumazi and a warrant for my arrest has been issued. Lilith is aware that you are here, in addition to other members of the Grigoric order and soon the whole of Heaven will know. I will attempt to hide you."

Janus drew back in fear. "Hide me, for what purpose?"

Raphael looked at the display and then his newfound friend and replied, "That you might lead those that will listen to your cause. Lilith, we both know manipulates the brothers. He only shows them a partiality of the vision given him during the Trial of Sight. He seeks to usurp me; to preserve his life. I am foreseen that he will indeed succeed in part. But he will not take you. For I will have you… sequestered."

Janus looked around and saw nothing but whiteness and the stone slab in the room. Even the tables which held the refreshments had disappeared and the slab itself slowly began to melt into the floor.

Raphael then raised his hands and spoke aloud, "Library."

Rows and rows of books then appeared on the walls and shittim wood shelves which reached the ceilings ascended as far as the eyes could see. A door then appeared in the distance that presumably exited the room.

"I apologize that I must inconvenience you my friend. I also wish we had more time to chat, but what I do now you will not understand, but you will understand hereafter." Raphael then spoke to the tome of Janus and said, "Collect thy author."

Immediately, Janus then felt himself dissolve; as if his very essence was being scattered, yet he could still somehow see his surroundings as he floated into his own book, and he, and the book: became one. Raphael then grabbed the tome and closed the book shut with a thud.

Janus then watched as Raphael placed his parchment bound tome on a nondescript shelf on the wall. And he spoke. "When I am gone, the room will return to its natural state. And you and your volume will separate and thou shalt be well. You will then come and find me, and if *I* be well, then I will come and find you, but if not. Know that I am given over to dissolution. Then you must use the room to gather my people and let them read what has transpired here. You must be prepared to take on the mantle of the Redactor of Raphael, and that of the Sephiroth of this realm. My eyes are hidden upon a pedestal atop the roof. Nebula guards them that none my take them save he that is worthy."

106

Raphael smiled, "I believe that thou art indeed worthy to succeed me and lead the people. Do this for me and fulfill the call placed on thee by the head of thy people in two realms." Raphael then ripped a page from his own tome hidden beneath his chest and placed it as an added page to that of Raphael Primes page and continued.

"You shall be called the Navigator of the Way. The one for whom the Mists will submit: the Two Faced One, and Redactor to two realms; he who can see beyond the God-sight to the realm of Limbo itself. Fear not this sight. For I have added my own page to the pages of your own realm's liege, that ye might be bridge between Alpha and Omega and complete the mission for which my counterpart hast called thee."

A hard knock came at the door and the floating angel turned towards it. "It is time for me to be betrayed."

Four Grigori then floated through the door and after they passed; the door exploded into pieces and Lucifer and Michael marched through with swords in hand, and Arelim warrior angels accompanied them.

Lucifer opened his mouth to speak. "In the name of the Lumazi of which I am chief, and by the authority invested in me.

Prince Raphael of House Grigori you are hereby placed under arrest. Will you come willingly or must we compel you to comply?"

Raphael looked at the Grigoric officers that floated and surrounded him. Their pens had turned into daggers. And they which comprised the company was Lilith Prime, Lilith Chi, and both Argoth and Janus of the Chi realm.

"Are you clear in your purpose?" Raphael asked the quartet.

Argoth was first to respond, "This one here has shown us a vision that cannot be denied. We do not wish to do thee harm, But our obedience to the Chief of Angels is clear."

Raphael nodded. "There is obedience yes, but then there is submission, which do you think is the greater?"

Argoth reflected upon Raphael's question and began to speak when Lucifer interrupted him and shouted. "Enough! We are not here to banter ethics with a traitor. Seize him and if he resists let his body see dissolution that the stone might be preserved."

Immediately, Lilith and Janus each took an arm and confiscated Raphael's pen and proceeded to led him out the room.

Argoth Chi did not move, and Lucifer and Michael saw his hesitation and spoke aloud their concern. "Does this action move thee to doubt?"

Argoth replied, "It is naught. The vision we have seen is sure. Nevertheless, when Raphael vacates this place, it will still need to be tended. I will stay and evaluate what intelligence can be gathered. Lilith is needed with you to evaluate the truth of the prince's words but someone must stay here."

Michael replied, "Your words bear wisdom. However, let two bear witness so that integrity might be maintained. Janus will also stay behind and assist you."

Argoth was tempted to object but knew that his hesitation made him suspect, and replied. "Let it be as you say."

Janus then bowed to the two princes, and both Liliths escorted Raphael out behind Lucifer and Michael.

And Janus; his spirit captured within his own tome by Raphael, watched as the angelic prince was led away in chains.

* * *

Argoth, Lilith-theta, and Lucifer-theta; had portaled and the three angels found themselves walking on lush grass, surrounded by various trees of beauty. Large palm leaves dripped dew and lanky red vines draped the canopy of the forest ceiling. Birds sang and the roars of great beasts sounded in the distance. Frogs and snarls of unseen things permeated the air in chorus with chirping insects that hugged the forest floor. The woodland was alive and awash in color and sound.

"Where are we?" Argoth asked.

Lucifer replied, "We are in the region of Eden. The garden which El has made is not far from here. But we dare not venture forth towards it for the man and the woman are there, and I would not have us bring our conflict to the shores of their home."

Lilith replied, "It would seem Raphael has done just that if we indeed abide on the outskirts of the human's domain."

Lucifer pointed towards a tree, and Argoth and Lilith each took Lucifer's arm around their shoulders and gingerly made their way towards the tree and laid him down.

Lilith noted that Lucifer was bleeding and was becoming

dizzy as they walked, and he watched as Lucifer collapsed into unconsciousness. The duo then gingerly laid him at the foot of a large oak tree.

"What is wrong with him?" Argoth asked.

Lilith laid the now unconscious Prince of Angels on his back and tore open Lucifer's robe to reveal a deep sword wound. Blood flowed from it in small geyser like spurts and Lilith immediately took Argoth's hand and placed it over the gash. "Keep your hand pressed over the wound and continue to apply pressure."

Argoth did as he was bidden while Lilith took a page from the back of his tome and slid it over Lucifer's flesh. The page melded into the skin of the angel and then disappeared.

Lilith frowned that the bleeding had slowed but it did not stop. Argoth noted his brooding demeanor. "What is wrong?"

"His flesh is not like all angels." Lilith replied. "He is covered with living precious gems; his skin texture changes. It will take time to apply the treatments needed to heal this wound as the injury cuts through multiple layers of his skin and is deep. Michael's blow was a strike meant to kill. You do understand this?"

Argoth observed Michael's handiwork. And it was indeed

a savage rend to the flesh that the prince had managed to perpetrate on Lucifer.

Argoth looked around, "Do what you can. I will scout the area."

He rose to fly away when Lilith grabbed his arm. "Are you soiled in the mind? Do it not!"

Argoth looked at him confused. "What? We need to see where we are and determine our next course of action."

Lilith theta frowned, "No, I know that you are Grigori, and I know that you are from what you call the Prime realm. But you and I both know that Grigori are assigned to all things. We do not know which of our people or how many of any given caste are for us, and how many are for our enemies. Raphael chose this place for a purpose. You are a Grigori; use your eyes: do you not see?"

Argoth frowned at the angel but did as bidden and looked to his left and right, and noted that Lilith was correct. There were no Grigori assigned to this area. He could see none of his people and he remarked hid observation. "It is a null."

"Yes," replied Lilith. "Raphael has not assigned orders to this area yet. With the ensuing conflict between Lucifer and Michael, and Michael waging war: he has sent us to a place that for the time being, we are safe from prying eyes. I do not know how long we have. For of a surety in time our people will find us: but for now… for now we are safe. Sit."

Argoth let out a small sigh of relief but only for a moment before he spoke. "I should not be here. You are not whom I am here to apprehend." Argoth looked at the Lilith before him and scoured the angel's person, looking up and down at his face and his clothing.

Lilith noted his gaze. "Yea, Redactor. I am not he whom you seek. But tell me…what has my counterpart done to warrant bounty for his arrest, that you would dare traverse Limbo to apprehend him?"

Argoth looked above his head once more and eyed the area to assure himself they were alone, and sat down a stones throw from the angel and replied. "In *my* world. *You* have betrayed the order of Grigori. In my world you have fled our realm to seek solace in another. To undo the vision cast given thee."

Lilith nodded, "Ah, I see. Yet, here I am… fleeing. It would seem Argoth, that our mutual choices would have your counterpart hunt me in my own realm as well. Now that Raphael is dead, it is only a matter of time before Argoth and others will search for us."

113

Argoth lowered his eyes away from Lilith in shame and re-flected. For he had not considered that he might encounter his own double in this realm: a double that would be influenced by the actors of this dimension. Would his counterpart help him?

Lilith noted his silent musing and spoke. "Yea, our people... many of the Host will seek us out. It is inevitable that we will in time be found. For who can hide from the angels of God? Mayhap, it *is* a good thing then that when I was called to lead house Grigori, I declined the nomination, on the grounds that others were more suitable to lead: for who knows that if I had partaken in the ritual; I too would have become outcast?"

Argoth shrugged his shoulders. "Perhaps, the thing is not known. But my heart can attune to the Lilith of my realm. If he is here I will be able to sense his presence."

Lilith-Theta frowned and replied, "Your sudden appearance would indeed explain much of the behavior that I have seen from both the princes and others."

"What do you mean? Do not hold back what is in thy mind. Speak freely," said Argoth.

Lilith applied another bandage to Lucifer's wound, sat down and wiped his brow. He took out his tome and flipped through several of its pages.

"There was an incident not long ago. An angel by the name of Abaddon was judged and condemned for the murder of another. He was lifted into a living mountain. A mountain created by El himself: a mountain that consumed angels alive. I was asked to minister as journal to the acts of Lucifer by Raphael and was away when this occurred. We were here tending to the details of El's Garden. And as was my duty, I wrote what I saw. The Prince's thoughts were conflicted. I had never seen such conflict, pride, yea arrogance even. I could sense that my charge was… changing; pursuing thoughts that if carried out would breed horror for us all. But something changed in him. I noted that at some point he looked at himself, and realized that he was the glory of the Father, and if he, being a creature could possess such beauty... if, he being just a son could possess all the Father had, how much more would he possess if he kept within the bounds of his Father's love? So I recorded Lucifer's heart as it battled to stay the course of fealty towards El. And when Lucifer had come back to the realm immortal to report of his progress, El eventually had taken a rest from all his work and had left the chief prince in charge. Lucifer then commanded that angels be stationed at Eden to assure El's will towards the humans. He even floated as a winged serpent among the trees and communicated with them. But when report was given that Michael needed to see him immediately we left Earth to return to Heaven and Michael was armed with a sword. A blade alive that could be unleashed against seven at one time and he commanded that Lucifer surrender himself for judgment. And when the Chief Prince refused Michael deemed him a traitor, and the Lumazi was split. Raphael then took Lucifer and portaled away. But Michael followed and the rest you know. I do not know how much of Heaven is in conflict. But Prince Raphael has bought us time to escape alive."

Argoth thought long and hard about their situation. "How long do you think it will be before Lucifer is healed?"

Lilith shrugged his shoulders. "The thing is hard to say. Who do you know among angelic kind to have ever tended to such a wound? Have those in your realm also succumbed to war, that you would know of these things?"

Argoth looked down and frowned. "I know not. Limbo obscures the river of time. But I do know that my realm also is in danger. I can only pray that my mission to apprehend the Lilith of my realm will ward off undue harm for my people."

Argoth suddenly collapsed to his knees and wave after waves of nausea came over him. "Why do I feel weak so suddenly?"

Lilith looked at him and spoke, "In your realm has El already begun his rest?"

Argoth shook his head as another flood of nausea came over him and he heaved phlegm from his mouth unto the ground; coughing to clear his throat. He wiped his sleeve with his shirt and spit the remnant of uncleanness from his mouth.

"If El still works in your domain, then consider yourself fortunate. For in this realm, the presence of El hast withdrawn. And with it the warmth and life which flows from the King that sustains us all. Your spasms are a living reminder that in Him we live, move and have our being. He is Life, and even his rest shakes the foundations upon which existence rests. It is an unnerving thing to know that God is not there: yes?"

Lilith slowly helped the angel to lay down at the base of a tree near Lucifer, and Argoth nodded. "Unnerving is an appropriate term."

Lilith stared at him. "I see that you are a Redactor. But your *sight* seems... hampered. Is the thing so?"

Argoth had not understood why he could not fully see. It took Lilith to let him know that the place was absent of Grigori. El's withdrawn presence impacted his powers. Or perhaps Limbo's

117

crossing. He just knew that as of this moment: he was partially blind.

"Aye, I am hampered in my vision. I cannot Trance."

Lilith eyed the angel and spoke, "Your mind races with thoughts of concern for Raphael and your realm. I see that you had vied to lead our house. Be still my friend and let me lead you into the Trance, and we shall see what the end shall be." Lilith-theta then stretched out his hand and offered it to Argoth.

Argoth allowed himself to settle down. He had just watched his friend killed by one of Heaven's chief princes: a person for whom he held the greatest respect. He now was in hiding with the injured Chief of Angels; who himself was being hunted for what he *might* do. And now, this one who extends his hands; was but another fashion of the angel he would have to find, apprehend, and bring back alive to avert a cataclysm to his own realm.

Thoughts raced through Argoth's mind. Could he trust this Lilith? How much were they *really* different? What differentiated this angel from the one he was sent to capture?

Could he trust his counterpart in this realm? What would be his judgment of the actions of Michael and what had transpired? Surely his self in all realities would do and see things as he sees them now?

"Argoth?" said Lilith-theta. "I see that a great many thoughts circle the sky of your mind. Know that I cannot answer the thoughts of your heart. I can however show you my own. Please... allow this steward to show himself faithful." Lilith then motioned for Argoth to take his hand.

Argoth looked at the angel and then took his hand into his.

Lilith smiled and then folded his legs across one another placing his foot on the opposite thigh. He then placed his hand over Argoth's head as if he would anoint him. His eyes turned white and his head tilted back as if he were staring into space.

Images then raced into his mind: images that cascaded also to Argoth.

A moving picture now played as they observed their waking dreams. For, a mountain named Hell was alive and ravenous for the flesh of angels. And the two watched Michael weave through the intestines of the creature until he arrived deep within the kiln, where he created a weapon to fight Lucifer Draco who was seen as a beast with seven heads. A red dragon that spewed flames and under whose command legions of Elomic armies marched to destroy their brothers. Kilnstones rained from the skies and God in his great wrath expelled Lucifer and many of the Host to parts across the universe both known and unknown.

Lilith grimaced in pain but he continued as the images marched before him unabated. Argoth watched as in his realm Lilith and Raphael fought with the former: only to die at the hands of his friend. Both angels' eyes began to well up with tears when it was seen that Raphael's fate was to be consumed alive by a stray kiln-stone.

Argoth felt himself grow angry; angry that the death of his friend was from the battle that ensued between the brothers Lucifer and Michael; angry because in the scale of their struggle his people were forced to remain unmoved, static and be witness to the chaos that surrounded them; angry because they had split Heaven into fac-tions.

And Lilith, locked with Argoth in their shared vision, knew the thoughts of his peer's heart and spoke. "Know and understand what shall befall thy people in the latter days: for yet the vision is for many days. But know that even whilst you are here. Thy land seethes with pride to obtain a station that can never be. For while my charge here sleeps and my twin attempts to undo what can only be the inevitable; save he repents. Your land *will* see war at the hands of Lucifer. He will march upon the temple and yea even bleed God.

But know that God hast ordained that this should be. To give space for the flowering of all his children's desires that he might know the heart of them. And even now, Raphael knows that Limbus has separated ye from he. And he will come and find thee, but you will never be the same, and the day upon which you lay eyes upon thy friend will be the last that thou shalt see him until El creates a new heaven and a new earth. But the vision is yet for an appointed time, but at the end it shall speak, and not lie: though it tarry, it will surely come, it will not tarry."

Lilith then settled from the Trance and floated to the ground and when he did Argoth stared at him with his mouth open.

"You have seen what will happen! How can you say this and tend to this one here?"

Lilith looked at Lucifer and replied. "*This* Lucifer before you now is not he who will kill Raphael. Nor is it he who sits before us now and leads angelic armies to overthrow El while he Sabbaths. No Argoth, it is Michael who marches across Heaven who searches for us, and though he hast not attempted to overthrow El. No doubt his actions are influenced by the poisoned consul of this Lilith from *your* realm. War nonetheless rages, for are we not split if some say I am of Lucifer and others Michael? I am glad I did not seek to lead.

But it matters now not. For our actions are our own. For in your realm war will come and civil war cannot be stopped. And in my realm civil war is already here because of a contagion that is from *your* realm. For, who art thou that judgest another man's servant? To his own master he stands or falls. Yea, this one here shall be holden up: for God is able to make him stand. Do not judge the actions of those who are before you unless you are prepared to judge your own. Do you think I hide from Michael alone; for though you hunt my counterpart: thy counterpart hunts us both. Have ye not already learned the lesson that should be evident? Are ye indeed blind not to just Grigoris sight but to the ways of El. For have ye not seen enough to know that these things are but ensamples? Should you not be admonished in seeing the paths that have been taken by so many? Wherefore let him that thinketh he standeth take heed lest he fall. Or do you deem yourself so far removed? For *my* Argoth will find us, and when he does: you will then be face to face with thine own face and the choices *you* have made in this realm."

Argoth was smitten by Lilith's words and replied. "I have made a grave error. I ask for forgiveness. If Lilith is the source of this realm's contagion then I am honor bound to see it undone. I will help if I can, but my charge to bring the rogue angel back is my first cause. I am clear in my purpose."

Lilith nodded, "It would seem that you are indeed. But *I* see that *you* see through a glass darkly. For example, have you even given thought on how you will escape this realm with Lilith?"

Argoth froze. He realized that his movements since he arrived did not give himself time to consider what if he did succeed? How would he get home? He then spoke aloud his solution.

"There is but one way to go; one place that can return me to my realm: the Gate of Limbus. And if Michael seeks Lucifer's life to forestall what he thinks will be an upcoming and larger war: then you and the Chief Prince must accompany me. For only there can we gain advantage if Heaven seeks the Chief Prince out: only *there* can we truly hide from our Grigoric brethren."

Lilith moved away from Argoth. "You would have us brave Limbo? It is off limits for a reason."

"Indeed, yet it remains the only place where we *can* go. Where in creation do you imagine we might hide from the Grigori save Limbus?"

Argoth waited for Lilith-theta to respond and Lilith-theta shook his head and shrugged his shoulders. "It is a bold plan of yours. To take us to the domain that runs adjacent to all creation."

Argoth nodded, "I see no other choice. When Lucifer is healed, we must travel to the gate. There is no other way and our hope lies in him. For if Heaven is divided then perhaps we can reduce damage to her populace by leading those that would see her harm to follow. Is it possible to open a portal into Limbo?"

Lilith's eyes searched the corners of his mind. "I am not sure if such a thing is possible let alone desired. It is said that there are *things* that live within the realm. Shades and ghosts of decisions both taken and those not. We could possibly disrupt the natural order."

Argoth looked at him and replied, "The natural order has already been disrupted; for you talk to an angel from another dimension and the Michael of this realm hunts his own brother. Civil war if not already aflame kindles with each action we and others take."

Lilith sighed, "But what of El? What of his presence? And what will be our state when he awakes from his rest?"

Argoth looked up into the sky and he wondered aloud the same thoughts now expressed aloud by Lilith and replied.

"I pray that when he moves to bring judgment on our actions. He will not extinguish us from the realm of existence."

124

Chapter Fourteen

Janus watched as both Argoth of the Chi realm and his own counterpart began to survey the Hall of Annals. Janus Chi lightly brushed the books that were laid out over the shelves; pulling volume after volume. Each represented a tome that was the recorded acts as depicted by the Grigoric race. And as far as the eye could see: shelves lined the great room.

"Have you been here before?" Janus Chi asked.

"No, have you?"

Janus Chi replied, "Neither have I, and I was under the impression the room was much more than a mere housing of collected tomes, but I should have…"

Immediately the room flashed in a great white light and for a moment both angels were blind, as their eyes adjusted to images that faded from their view. Each rubbed their eyes to bring their sight into focus and when they looked up, there was nothing but white. White splayed over ivory and bleached in the color of alabaster. Where formerly a door was seen there no longer existed a door. No floor, nor ceiling, and naught could be seen but a small dark object which seemed like a book a mere ten feet before them.

Argoth-Chi looked about him befuddled. "What has happened and are we still within the Hall?

Janus-Chi shrugged his shoulders and also looked suspiciously at their surroundings, then spoke his own query out loud. "Where are we?"

Immediately, the room flashed and colors paraded themselves across the floor and ceiling. And on each walls were panoramic views of Heaven and all of her surroundings and the two angels noted that they were in a portion of the heavenly palace that was off limits to all but the Chief of Eyes, and they could see that they were within the tower of the great mansion that was El's house.

A rushing wind then entered the room and a small vortex swirled from the dark book that laid within the floor.

Argoth-Chi pointed at the tome and both eyed it as its pages flipped from front to back.

Slowly the tome disappeared and from it formed an angel... a Grigori. But the two observers noted that he stood larger and with a build different from others of their kind, and

126

that he possessed two faces: one black and the other white. And as he rose from the midst of the whirlwind, a tome hovered over him and a blue fiery sword emerged where a stylus would be the norm, and it invisibly moved and settled within the center of the angel's back. And when the Grigori looked at them with his two faces, he looked at them with four eyes. And two were a blazing white, set within the black face; and the others were as dark as onyx set within the white face.

Both angels then took a battle stance and their pens transformed into daggers.

Janus looked upon then and stretched out his hand and their tomes were pulled from their chests and each immediately collapsed to the ground. The two volumes raced through the air into his waiting hands and Janus plucked each from the air then placed them down at his feet.

He then spoke.

"I am Janus of House Grigori, Servant to the Living God and now Redactor to the Sephiroth of two realms. I am the Navigator of the Way and the One for whom the Mists will submit: the Two Faced One. I bridge the gap between Alpha and Omega. I have come to apprehend the renegade

Lilith of the Prime realm. You are invited to come and bear witness to the ascension of this one as Sephiroth. Collect your tomes if you would truly serve God. Or, die without record and I will give your tomes to others more worthy… now choose."

Immediately, Argoth and Janus-Chi crawled on their hands and knees, each wheezed as they dragged themselves towards Janus Prime and took their tomes and placed them back into their chests. They panted taking in great gulps of air as if recovering from suffocation and then bowed their heads to Janus. Janus-Chi looked up to look upon Janus and recognized that the face, while different; was his own and he spoke.

"You… you are me?"

Janus's two faces nodded. "No. Janus, you are you, and I am but a choice that you did not take. But since you do not understand the way of Limbus…" Janus then shook his head. "Yes, I am you."

Argoth-Chi opened his mouth to speak. "Why does your body language speak different than your words?"

Janus cocked his head in curiosity. "Does it?"

128

He then looked above him and spoke, "Nebula hast arrived, and we must go."

Janus then spoke aloud to the room, "Take me to the roof."

Immediately, the chamber changed and a hallway with stairs stood to his front, and the dark robed angel grabbed the stair rail, and proceeded to walk up towards the roof of the tower. He reached the ceiling then pushed against a wooden door and stepped onto the roof of the stone tower. He walked towards a pedestal and upon them sat two floating eyes.

A cloud then descended from the sky and slowly transformed into a humanoid figure of mist and spoke. "Welcome, Navigator of the Way. Raphael and I have been expecting you."

Janus tilted his head in both acknowledgment and a show of respect but remained silent.

Both Argoth and Janus-Chi had also made their way to the roof, and they too bowed in respect when they saw Nebula. "Are we come to witness the Trance Nebula?" Argoth-Chi asked.

Nebula sighed, "No, Grigori. You have come to bear witness that this one here… will become Sephiroth and will herald House Grigori into war."

Both Janus and Argoth Chi looked upon Janus with opened mouths in shock.

* * *

Lucifer-Chi circled Raphael, and the angel floated motionless as the Chief Prince paced around him.

"Do you know where the trespasser is?" Lucifer asked.

Raphael-Chi nodded, "I do."

"So then you acknowledge that he is a trespasser?" said Lucifer.

Raphael-Chi smiled and eyed Lilith Prime. "I admit that he is no different from this one here; one, who has traversed the gate of Limbo, while this to your side claims to be Grigori, but in truth, is a manipulator here to serve his own ends. At least the traveler that I know honors our King.

I also acknowledge that *he* serves El, as do we all. Or have *you* forgotten whom you serve?"

Lucifer winced at the remark. "I am very much aware of my responsibilities, both to the Lord and to the kingdom. And I will not see it sullied with infiltrators who come to do the realm harm."

Raphael tilted his head in surprise and spoke softly. "Do you think that your handling of me *honors* God?"

Raphael then turned to see Michael with his head down and spoke to the Prince of Kortai. "And what of you Michael... will *you* stand by and watch this travesty of justice? Will *you* be complicit in this act? Or have you also joined in the suspension of the Parliament of Angels, that you would follow this rebellion that even now has time to be stopped?"

Michael was sullen and put his hand on Lucifer's shoulder and whispered *into* Lucifer's ear. "Brother... a word?"

Lucifer eyed Raphael and followed Michael where they could speak out of earshot.

Michael opened his mouth to speak, and he carefully measured his words. "Brother, he is Lumazi. Raphael has been appointed by God himself to lead the Grigori. If we continue in this trial, I dare say we risk fracturing the Lumazi. Have not enough breaches been incurred already with the Schism? Would you see us create a rift even further than our current separation from the Seraphim and Ophanim?"

Lucifer looked at Michael and his face grew stern. "I am the Chief Prince. I stand in the stead of God whilst He rests. I will not see Creation tainted with foreign influencers who seek to tear down our realm. I am the Chief Prince and I too am also appointed by God. My will is law and if Raphael continues in his defiance. I will strip him of his title and give his house to another. And if his title is not enough to release the truth from his lips, I will see him to the gates of dissolution and feed him to Hell. You are either for me or against me. Or do you seek to challenge me in this thing?"

Michael bowed, "Nay brother... my prince. No I do not. El has made his decision clear. You are the first among us and where you lead, I will follow. Nevertheless, you are not the conservator of Heaven. Be careful lest you raise the ire of the house of Elohim, for all may not obey a call to action if they fear such a call would rebel against the revealed will of El."

Michael, frustrated with his brother then turned to walk away and brushed against Lucifer and headed back towards Raphael and spoke.

"Tell him what he needs to know… please. For, I do not wish to see you harmed."

Raphael smiled. "Be not alarmed for my welfare for I have seen a vision. And I am sorry for what I have seen. Alas, it is too late for me now. I will see my end soon. For even as we speak a hardness of heart concretes itself within Lucifer's bosom. But you — your end is not to be. For I have seen that there are worse things than dissolution. For *you* Michael of the Kortai will have power to act but will also fall away. And in the end, will live to love what is thine true love. But your love will turn to ash; for the hatred wherewith you shall hate, shall be greater than the love wherewith you once loved."

Michael then stepped away from Raphael and was afraid, for his words were laced in both sorrow and conviction of a future yet to come.

Lucifer at that moment intervened, and he brushed Michael aside and looked at Raphael. "I shall play your game brother. Lilith... attend me."

Both Lilith's came to Lucifer side, and he smiled. "You see Raphael. I have not one but two Grigori concerned that the truth of thy record be told."

Lucifer then looked at them both and queried them. "This one here will not surrender the secrets with which he holds. Can you withdraw his record that we might see?"

Lilith Chi replied, "It is not for us to reveal the mysteries of house Grigori to non-Grigori, only El may reveal the contents of the Book of Life."

But Lilith Prime interjected and replied. "Yea, the thing can be done."

Lilith-Chi looked at him and scowled shaking his head disapprovingly. Lucifer then looked at Lilith and then Lilith-Chi, smiled then walked towards Lilith.

"Lilith of House Grigori; speak that this one here may also speak. Tell me what I need to know. You claim to have come to prevent a war that cannot be stopped. Tell me what I desire and I will use all within my power to minimize the impact of this war."

Lilith then looked at Raphael and spoke aloud. "He is the Sephiroth. He cannot be forcibly made to reveal his secrets. For Raphael is the journal of the Almighty himself. You cannot destroy the journal of God. And the words within are sealed up so that none in Heaven are worthy even to read what is written therein. For, the word of the Lord abides forever. Thus, Raphael carries El's tome. The angel's very heart is His written word. But his body... this flesh which surrounds the Book of Life does not. It is but a shell which carries the tome. But if the body be destroyed, the tome will be free to be read. But beware, for it not a trite thing to think yourself worthy to unseal what God hast sealed. But yea, if the body is destroyed then indeed the seals may be snapped and the musings of God available to be read."

Raphael raised his eyebrow and looked at Lilith Prime knowingly. Lilith eyed the angel then smirked and rolled his eyes and a condescending smile arose on his face.

Lucifer eyed his brother's body language and scrunched his shoulders and spoke. "He is living mist at will.

As are all your kind. How then do we destroy his flesh?"

Lilith looked at Raphael and smiled at him as he replied to Lucifer. "What shalt you render to me? What reward will be given to dispense this one and surrender his tome to thee?"

Lucifer looked at him and then at Lilith-Chi of his own realm. "I will deed you his house, and all those under his charge and when I have acquired the knowledge of the tome needful to find this impostor from another realm, then I shall petition the Lord that the book be yours to hold."

Lilith-Chi appealed to him, "But my prince! This one here is not even of this realm! What of Janus, Argoth and yes even I who have served House Grigori and were selected by the people?"

Lucifer looked at Lilith-Chi and replied, "Will thou surrender to me the knowledge contained within the Book of Life?"

Lilith-Chi stood mute and downcast and turned his face away.

Lucifer nodded, "Because thou hast refused to convey what I need, therefore you are stripped of rank and title. For how can I expect the people to follow thee, when *you* will not follow me? Away from my sight, for I have use of those who will help me achieve my ends. And you have made clear that this will *not* be thee."

Lilith-Chi stood humbled before his twin, Raphael, Michael and Lucifer. The angel then turned with a bowed head to go. He began to exit the room and looked at Raphael who stood silent and shook his head disapprovingly. Slowly he closed the wooden door as it creaked behind him and left Raphael-Chi to his fate.

Lilith then stood in front of Raphael-Chi and spoke. "Now… let us begin the extraction."

Raphael smiled. "I am the Sephiroth. I see with the eyes of God: do you think because El Sabbaths that your works are not known to Him? I am the eyes of God. I *see* with the eyes of God. Even in his rest El sees you. When you slumber He hears thee; for the Lord's presence is every-where, and the number of hairs on thy very head is known to the king. For if thou would ascend up into the heights of Heaven, he is there: and if thou would make thy bed in hell, behold, He is there. And lo, there is nothing covered that shall not be revealed. Nor hidden that will not be made known. Raphael then misted and the chains which bound him fell to the ground: for he chose to be bound no longer.

Lucifer immediately detonated into light in an attempt to blind the angel and all those within his presence covered their eyes but Raphael remained unmoved. "I am the eyes of the Lord. You cannot blind me Draco. You reach to obtain knowledge that is not yours to possess, and *you* will not have it."

Raphael quickly dug within his chest to reveal its tome. He took his pen and stabbed the pulsating book. He immediately began to dissolve into nothing, and like ash is blown into the wind. The Book of Life also began to slowly dissolve into nothing.

Lilith seeing what Raphael-Chi had done then immediately reached into his folds and pulled the Kilnstone that controlled time and drew upon its power. A wave of green light expanded from his person and concentric waves of temporal power flowed from him and Raphael-Chi and all within the chamber were caught within the expanding bubble.

Raphael was gone. But the book stood phased between two states of being: present but was not: suspended. Almost ethereal in its appearance it floated as Lilith focused the God-stone's power to keep the object from blinking out of existence. He motioned with his hands and the green envelope of temporal power coalesced around the book alone.

Lucifer-Chi looked at him as did Michael and he spoke to Lilith. "What has happened? What did he do, and what are you doing?"

Lilith grimaced as he attempted to keep the book from following its master. "Raphael has sacrificed himself. Another... somewhere is now become the Sephiroth, and the Book of Life now strains to go to its new master. Somehow Raphael has picked another successor to the book. And while I cannot stop this transition, I can with this God-stone forestall it. The stones power counters the Book of Life and prevents it from phasing to its new master: but it fights me. I cannot reverse what Raphael has done. But I can curb the rate of which it occurs. But it is the book of El, and I do not know if I can keep it within this realm or even this point in time. If you desire the book, you must find to whom it is being summoned. I am now forced to stay here to attend to it lest our efforts be in vain. I can prolong its vanishing mayhap a day, but not longer. If you wish to do this thing before El awakes then you must go. Now hurry if you wish to find him who would be its new home."

Lucifer then turned, and his twelve wings which draped his person flowed about him as a cape. He walked past his brother Michael and spoke. "You are with me."

Michael nodded, and he too turned to leave with his brother and they exited the throne room and proceeded to vacate the temple itself when they looked into the sky and a blue light showed a Grigori unlike any they had ever seen and Janus Prime looked down upon them with a blue sword and was making pronouncement to all of Heaven.

* * *

Janus looked upon the floating pedestal that held Raphael's two eyes. He was hesitant to reach out to them and Nebula, Argoth and Janus-Chi watched him and understood his hesitation.

Nebula then spoke, "If you take the eyes of another; their vision will be yours. Raphael has prepared me to witnesses this Grigori. He would see one from another realm; would lead the house of Grigori through the coming conflict ahead. He has foreseen your coming and has selected you to lead but do you consent?"

Janus looked at the eyes. He was the Redactor to Raphael in his realm and now Redactor to Raphael-Chi. He gazed as the floating pupils which gazed back at him... waiting. For, with the taking of Raphael-Chi's eyes he would become something more than any Grigori had ever seen or become: Navigator of the Way; The Two Faced One, He who could see into all realms.

He reached out to touch them and Nebula spoke. "Take heed great one. Do not reach for them unless you verbally consent. For with confession is the thing heard in Heaven. Consent that you will give: an eye... for an eye. Because El is at rest, the transaction cannot be made, save you surrender of thy own free will—thine eyes. Raphael in his wisdom would cause thee to exact a price if you would lead House Grigori and walk in the paths that El Pneuma treads. El will honor this exchange, but only if you confess.

Are you ready?"

Janus shook his head as he absorbed the ramifications of taking the sight to lead house Grigori. He swallowed hard and replied. "Yes."

"Do you desire to see with the eyes of God?" Nebula asked.

Janus closed his eyes and replied, "Yes."

Nebula then asked for a third time. "Do you truly love the Lord thy God that thou would see what he sees and cease to see with thine own eyes."

Janus eyes were closed, and he was still and whispered, "Yes."

Nebula then lifted the two floating eyes that Raphael had given to God as a token of his fealty, and he held them aloft before Janus and spoke. "Then if thine eye offends thee... pluck it out."

Argoth-Chi's brow narrowed as he quivered thinking about what he was about to witness.

Janus nodded then spoke aloud for his words to be

heard, "So be it."

He then placed his palms flat against his face. He took a deep breath then quickly curled his fingers inward into the sockets of his eyes and clawed them out.

Argoth and Janus Chi winced and turned away as Janus Prime screamed out in agony.

Blood spewed from his face and moans echoed over the rooftop of the palace; moans that floated upon the clouds of Heaven and into the earshot of the Host within the heavenly city.

Nebula hovered over to Janus and the living cloud then reached into Janus's hands and took his clawed out eyes and placed them on the altar. He then took Raphael's eyes and gave them to Janus and spoke. "Take what thou hast earned and see with new eyes."

Janus then took the eyes given him and gently placed them into his sockets. Immediately his face was healed, and he blinked for the vision he beheld was wondrous to behold, and the angel could see into all realms and he could somehow follow the path of all decisions: to see the outcome of every decision. Yet, unlike El who saw all things at once.

Janus still needed time to scour the tree of time and explore the various branches of all things. Thus the angel became Sephiroth and was given the God-sight: a sight unlike any in creation, but yet short of the omniscience of God himself. For while El could explore all realities at once to their immediate end; past present and future. Janus could only do so consecutively over time.

Nebula then spoke into the ears of Janus and Argoth Chi. "Behold the head of house Grigori. Navigator of the Way and the Two Faced one."

Both Janus and Argoth bowed before their new head.

"But what of Raphael?" Argoth asked.

Nebula smiled and spoke to Janus, "Raphael are you there?"

Janus turned and smiled. "We are both here."

Nebula nodded, "Then what we have seen has begun. And the conflicts to ensue over obedience to unlawful commands will escalate. For some will refuse to submit and will be sentenced to Hell." Nebula sighed, "Lucifer and Michael act in thought that they do the will of God but have become increasingly blind that they will soon set out to destroy his works. It is only a matter of time before they will think that the yoke of El itself is too much to bear."

Janus looked into the distance, "The choices of these two I can see in Limbo. The repercussions of which can no longer be stopped. Nevertheless, we must act while choices yet remain for us to do so. For in this realm I have foreseen the end; for Lucifer hast not just in this realm sought to rebel against his king, but seeks to abscond with the knowledge of the thoughts of God. And when El awakes, he will not just exile for this treachery but shall in his wrath destroy all sentient life save man."

Janus then turned to Argoth-Chi and his dimensional counterpart. "I am sorry that war will come to your realm. I am sorry that I must lead House Grigori through this upcoming tumult. Do not think that war is upon you to fight for victory over thy brothers. For, if you think our cause is for this, then you are sorely mistaken. For, know that the war that we must now fight is to prevent our extinction. I have now seen this inevitability. Even now I search the choices that solidify every moment we stand here... choices that cannot be undone. I can see this... Lucifer does not; for the Lilith

145

of my realm hast once again weakened the barriers between dimensions and Limbo shudders to restrain what lies within. We must attend to this or none of our realities will be safe. For the Grigori are the needle that binds in El's name the threads of reality. We must repair the breach that Lilith's actions have caused. Nebula, I must rally House Grigori. Grant me the sky please."

Nebula nodded, and he sang a song in a language other than Elohim, and the sky became as a mirror and Janus then floated into the sky and he took from his chest the tome of his heart… a book that changed every second to become the Book of Life. And it beat erratically as if pages were being added yet somehow withheld. And Janus, knew that Raphael-Chi's gambit to prevent Lucifer-Chi's capture of the Book of Life by transferring his spirit to dwell with his own: was in partial abeyance. The angel lifted his hands and his image filled the sky and he spoke to the host of Heaven.

"Lucifer Draco of house Draco. You have no need to search for the home of the Book of Life. For, I am here, and will soon be… there." Janus pointed to the light filled tunnel that was Limbo.

"You seek me? To know the intent for which I have come? Very well. Know that it is to apprehend the one that holds my pages in suspension. Know that I will indeed seize him and see him return to the realm of my birth. Know also that your paths are known to me and that the omniscience that you seek will be denied thee.

Know that thine actions have given me pause in the fulfillment of my mission; for thou art beside thyself and have forgotten whence thou wast taken. For, when thou wast little in thine own sight, wast thou not made the head of the tribes of El, and did not the Lord anoint thee prince over his people? But now thy wisdom and thy knowledge hath perverted thee; and thou hast said in thine heart, I am, and none else beside me. And now those true to the House of Grigori will abide thy pride no longer. No longer will the works of creation be published. For on this day we will pause the pens of our kind and leave Heaven for her defense. For house Grigori, will not be complicit in thy collusions against our king.

Therefore, here me O'house Grigori! The Lord thy God is one God, and who is this Lucifer Draco that he would defy the dictates of our God? Come to me and we shall depart this place, and let those that dare stop us know that House Grigori now secedes from the Parliament of Angels! For our cause is to the word of God itself, and to that cause I bid all clans come that we might shore up the realms of existence."

Janus then turned his eyes to Lucifer and Michael-Chi who stood by his side and made pronouncement. "You desire me *Light-bringer*? Then follow me if you dare."

Janus then opened a portal to the basement of Heaven. And Nebula mirrored all so that all in Heaven could see what the new head of House Grigori had done. And Janus had disappeared and now stood before the shimmering blue gate of Limbo. And both Argoth and Janus-Chi stood with him and the three walked through the foggy mirror-like Gate.

The air of Heaven then shimmered and thousands of Grigori could be seen floating and visible to all. Blue portals opened up above and below them, and the glittering doorways were everywhere the eye could see. And all manner of angels watched as House Grigori floated in droves into the portal of Limbo, and none dared to stop them for they wrote the doings of all things.

And Lucifer looked into the skies and was incensed that below his feet in the basement of the temple; House Grigori seceded and left the realm to venture forth into Limbo.

And Lucifer looked at Michael and commanded, "Rally the Host. I will not have the Parliament splintered. We will bring them to heel by force. And the Book of Life I will have. Now go and I will visit Eladrin that the Gate to Limbus be expanded that we might pass through and return them all."

Michael stared at his brother in disbelief over what he was hearing and he voiced his concern in fear and trembling.

"Lucifer you are leading Heaven into war."

Lucifer stood stone faced as he watched the Grigori depart Heaven, and his response to Michael was short and laced in bitterness. "Then there will be war. Now go — and be about thy princes business."

Michael bowed and went to assemble the remainder of the Lumazi and Host for battle.

Jerahmeel had been looking for his friend for several hours and it was unlike Raphael to not show for their morning communion. The whole Lumazi seemed on edge. Lucifer had been sent planet-side to for a task only known to him and El; while the rest of the council questioned the implications of Apollyon's query of the Lord's goodness. Jerahmeel could use a cup of Honey-bell Tea and enjoy some manna leaf in the company of his friend.

He walked from the upper level of the temple and made his way past the main entry way to depart the throne room when a shimmering blue light caught his eye. A sparkling blue mist seemed to creep across the floor and his eyes followed the source of the fog. He walked the path of the azure gloom and he found himself heading towards the basement of Heaven.

Down winding stone stairs he roamed until a glowing blue light penetrated around the corner; light that flickered as iridescent beams that bounced through still water. The Prince of Harrada peered around the corner of a wall to see Raphael: his arms were spread wide and raised, and with his hands he gestured in the air in fluid-like movements. His pen, was at his command covering over fissures that emanated every second from a glowing blue light-

150

ed doorway. And fog swirled around the angel whilst his tome was opened as its pages flapped through the air as if by a great wind and sheets were being torn out and flew into the shimmering gate.

Jerahmeel looked into the deep blue of the glowing doorway and power pulsed from it and through the mirror-like opening he could see himself smiling back at him while other humanoid figures crawled over the threshold from the other side as if they were searching for exit to escape. A dark figure lurked also in the center. He wore a crown, and even Jerahmeel could see that the figure looked menacingly at Raphael and the being simply stood there while the others of his kind slammed themselves into the invisible gate only to dissipate into mist then re-materialize behind their master.

Raphael stood working feverishly sealing up any cracks that instantaneously manifested. Jerahmeel could hear the whine of the gate as if it was vibrating and its pitch was slowly raising in volume even as the seconds passed while he observed. Alarmed at the sight he raised his voice to his brother.

"Raphael, what is going on here?"

Raphael turned to see that Jerahmeel was behind him and when he did a fissure went unsealed and a mist seeped from behind the mirror and moved with swiftness and scampered towards Raphael and a figure, then materialized in front of him and it smiled with teeth but no face, and it was ignited in blue flame.

Raphael turned back around and immediately pages from his book lifted from the tome and flew towards the creature mummifying it and it fell to the ground with a thud. The creature squirmed along the floor encased in the papyrus from Raphael's tome.

Raphael's pen had turned into a dagger and the blade that hovered near his ear dashed towards the thrashing body and in repeated downward strokes stabbed the enveloped creature. The form of the body then collapsed leaving nothing but a heap of crumpled papers. The leaflets then lifted from the floor and covered the fissure until they too melded and disappeared into the shimmering wall of energy.

Raphael turned his face back to the glowing gate and more of the humanoid gaseous creatures pounded against the barrier and in its center still stood the crowned misty persona at their locus. His eyes, a brimming yellow.

"Jerahmeel come to me... hurry," said Raphael.

Jerahmeel rushed to his friend's side, "What can I do?"

Raphael grimaced as an explosive wave of power hit the gate

from the other side and Raphael was pushed back unto his knees but his hands were still up; as if he was keeping the opening from bursting open.

Jerahmeel helped him to his feet and Raphael while rising did not take his eyes off the Gate but spoke to his friend "Jerahmeel there is a breach in the barrier that separates the realms. I must enter Limbo and restore the seals that hold its denizens in check."

Jerahmeel looked at him curiously and replied, "What denizens? Is not Limbo but the way to Aseir? A way now blocked by El?"

Raphael looked at his brother through the periphery of his eye, "Nay, our choices have populated the realm: the manifestations of alternate choices reside here. He that stands at its center is King: the first choice; a choice to run counter to El. It is he that empowers them all."

Jerahmeel looked at the gate and ghostly figures ran and flew rampant into the barrier that separated the domains. Humanoid mist like persons who dissipated as soon as they hit the glass; each creating a shockwave: a shockwave… and a fissure.

"What do they want?" Jerahmeel asked.

Raphael looked at he who stood at the center of the Mists and replied. "To feed, to be free, and to conform this world into the image of the choices we have said no to. I need to enter and stop the Mist King within his domain. I cannot stand here and forever keep the way to the gate. He must be dwelt with. Reasoned with... I will need you to stay here and guard the way. They cannot be allowed to pass."

Jerahmeel panicked. "Me? How am I alone to stop that onslaught?"

Increasing radiant waves of power crackled over the gate, and it glowed. And the hum from the waves; were like when a tuning fork is strummed. And more fissures crisscrossed the mirror like aperture of the gate.

Raphael then reached into his robe and pulled out his Kilnstone. It looked like a tome and he reached for Jerahmeel's hand and placed it within his palm. "You will use this. If the gate fails smash, the stone into the earth and it will shatter. It will release me and my life-force will obliterate all things around me. For the word of the Lord is life and I am his journal."

"Wait!" said Jerahmeel. "What will happen to you if I smash the stone?"

Raphael took off his robes and tightened his belt, preparing himself for the transition into Limbo. He then turned and placed his hand on Jerahmeel's broad shoulders and replied.

"I will die. But my life is not my own, for I am but the construct of the imagination and the will of God. Do not dissuade me with what I must do. For, I go to retrieve several of the Grigori that are currently adrift within the realm. Their presence has alerted the Mists to this domains weakness. El's power alone would normally make my presence unnecessary. But the removal of his immediate presence weakens the fabric of reality. And reality is deciding if it shall conform to El's design or determine one of its own. I must convince it to remain faithful to El. To bring it into remembrance that we are all servants and to whom we yield ourselves servants to obey, the servant are we to whom we obey; weather to sin unto death or of obedience unto righteousness. For, the time when El seems most far requires us to remain most faithful. And I am the Lord's servant and will not abandon Creation to degeneration."

Jerahmeel nodded in understanding. "Then do not die and bring our people home but should we not call the other Lumazi?"

Raphael turned towards the pulsating gate; its vibrations increasingly becoming more constant. "There is no time; for if you must smash my kilnstone and if El has not returned from his rest. There will be no need to inform the Lumazi; for all of Heaven will be invaded with imaginations solidified from this alternate realm and it shall be known among all that we are overrun. There will be pages that will leave my tome and head into the gate. If the last page is used bring all of Heaven to this gate for we shall be invaded. For Limbo will then be the source of a fire that must at all costs be doused: do you understand me?"

Jerahmeel nodded.

Jerahmeel watched as the cloud like creatures continued to assault the gate coming in throngs and flashes of light that beat upon the glowing door more and more. And the ferocity of the attack upon the portal made him begin to unconsciously rock. Jerahmeel looked at the activity of those that entered his world and his voice quivered. "Raphael, what *exactly* lies beyond the gate?"

"Unselected choices that now seek flesh… now stand back."

Jerahmeel did as bidden and when he took several steps away from Raphael. The head of house Grigori lifted his hands and his dagger quickened into his right hand and two sheets from his book which was now with Jerahmeel ripped from the journals binding and elongated into a transparent wall behind Raphael yet in front of Jerahmeel.

Jerahmeel watched his friend and saw him mouth the words, "El, give thy servant strength."

"Raphael!" Jerahmeel cried.

Raphael focused on the path set before him: sprinted with dagger in hand towards the pulsating gate and leaped into the entrance.

A brilliant flash pulsed from the entrance and a wave of bluish and white light escaped from where Raphael entered and darted through the room; temporarily blinding Jerahmeel and he dropped to his knees.

The angel covered his eyes and as vanishing silhouetted images of his surroundings dissipated from his temporary blindness. He rubbed his eyes to see that the gates fractures had been sealed and a lone humanoid figure with a crown examined with his hands the contour of the gate from its side. The entity eyed the angel as if inspecting him and scowled. Tentacles could be seen in the background behind him. Wings extended from him and he turned into the darkness and gloom and disappeared.

Jerahmeel raised himself from the ground and in front of him a shimmering wall of power stood between him and the entrance to Limbo. He too took his hand and began to touch the wall until the heat made him draw it back.

A small fissure appeared in the crack of Raphael's wall and a slight sizzle emanated from the barrier. Jerahmeel looked as another page ripped from the Grigori's tome flew from its bindings and dissipated into the barricade: slowing the spider like crack.

Jerahmeel armored himself and the thought occurred to him that he needed to fashion himself a weapon.

Chapter Fifteen

Lucifer-Chi made his way to the throne of the Ophanim and landed within the Aerie.

Hundreds of flying Ophanim looked at him and some spoke.

"The chief angel is here?"

"What does Kilnborn desire with Ophanim?"

"Hath this one not caused enough trouble?"

"Rewind him," said one.

Lucifer continued his procession undeterred towards the King of the Ophanim.

Escorted by two electrified balls of living lightning, each crackled and small bolts of plasma arced in front of the angel as an ever-present reminder that he was in the presence of those gifted by God to arbitrate times and seasons: the ones upon whose backs the constellations moved.

Lucifer approached the throne of Eladrin-Chi and bowed. The great ancient being lifted into the air; a circular ball of lightning, surrounded his person with gyrating rings that swiveled in several directions around his body; each wheel never touching the other.

Each ring contained eyes that faced a four faced being. And the voltaic creature spoke.

"With what cause does the Chief Prince of Angels stand before the King of the Ophanim?"

Lucifer stood unmoved by the spectacle before him and replied. "I request passage for the host to travel to the land of Limbo."

Eladrin looked upon Lucifer and replied, "The way to Aseir is forbidden. For thou and thy kind have made schism with the Seraphim. What thou ask I cannot do."

Lucifer then knelt before Eladrin and pressed his case further. "I do not seek passage to Aseir Great One. Nor do my people intend to breach the shores of the fire lands. But there are some who have defied the Parliament of Angels and have sought sanctuary within Limbus. This action cannot stand. Therefore, I go to lead my armies and to recover those who have seceded and reunite my people under a single banner. I need only a gate wide enough to take a legion into the realm."

Eladrin's giant rings slowed and Lucifer could see the glyph like tattoos that the Lord had written by hand upon the living wheel within a wheel.

160

Each of the twenty-four letters of the Elomic alphabet wrapped themselves around his two rings. Eladrin was the living gate to all realms. The localized being who could travel everywhere at once. Upon his shoulders the Lord had placed the responsibility of times and seasons. From the rotation of stars to the movement of galaxies, Eladrin and his people moved at the will of the Lord to do his bidding; creations who were reflective of God's power, wisdom and presence. The four faces of Eladrin turned and spoke as one.

"Why Lucifer Draco do I foresee blood and death in your future?" said the Eagle's face.

"Why art thou not content to abide in thy calling?" queried the face of the man face.

"Know that if you do this thing… to hunt thine own people…" warned the bear face.

"… your own stone may very well become darkened." the Ox face said.

Lucifer guffawed and rebuffed him. "Will you grant me passage for my cause or no? Or do you declare yourself to be in breach of your duty to carry my people when summoned?"

The four faces of Eladrin frowned and replied. "We will

abide by our duty to carry thee; even if it be to thine own demise. If a gate thou so desire. A gate thou shalt have: so be it."

Eladrin'-Chi's rings then spun and he and Lucifer disappeared and then reappeared at the portal of Argoth.

The great King of the Ophanim then turned upon himself and spoke. "Know that you will wrought folly in this act," said the Eagle face.

"Folly will surely come to you," said the Bear face

"The denizens of Limbo will not tolerate your presence," warned the Ox face.

"Gather your host Chief Prince." They all said as one, "And when you are ready. I will open a portal."

* * *

Henel James sat fascinated over the words that came from Argoth's mouth. Questions upon questions raced through his mind. But one question above all others rose to the top.

"You actually spent time with Lucifer? You mean to tell me that you protected *him*. Sheltered *him*?"

Henel shook his head as he mentally wrestled with questions which wrought confusion and dismay, "But why? Didn't you not know what he would eventually become?"

Argoth sighed and responded as he looked out a window into the great library and poured himself more honey-ale.

"No, son of James, I did not *know*." Argoth was quiet for a second and turned from looking out his window to turn to Mr. James and tilted his head in waiting. "But we both know the question that you desire to ask me... so ask."

Henel also breathed in deeply and released his thoughts into the air for review. "Would you... would you have killed him had you known?"

Argoth nodded, "I have at times wondered of my own past; wondered about the choices given me. Such is the pondering that comes with the complexities of Limbo. But such is also the way of God. When you consider His ways; consider that Yeshua when he walked the Earth in flesh once fed five thousand souls. Often I have found that your people have been far too quick to read though the biblical scrolls of the encounter; often, too simple and occupied to consider those that were ministered by him. For was it not Yeshua who spoke so long in discourse that *He* kept the people in his presence for so long that they eventually grew hungry? Consider when his disciples came to him did they not ask him to allow the people to depart that they might obtain food?"

Henel pondered Argoth's words and replied. "This is true. My memory of the scriptures tell me that he told the disciples no. Yeshua had the people remain where they were."

"Indeed, Mr. James, he told them no. So consider Mr. James that Yeshua was aware of the people's need for food yet for a time kept them hungry and even denied his disciples reasonable request to have the people leave. Now consider the ways of Yeshua Mr. James and be wise. Could not Yeshua have fashioned food needed from the dust of the earth by each family? Could he not have but spoke and the molecules in the air themselves would at his command fashioned wheat if he so desired?"

Henel nodded as he mentally recalled the gospel account of the story. He thought to himself and spoke aloud. "Yeshua is the Word made flesh. Of course he could have done whatever he desired."

Argoth nodded, "Exactly, but instead he utilized the people present and the resources *they* brought with them to do a miracle. He positioned *them* so they were dependent on the one thing that only he alone could give them... a miracle. He allowed them to experience faith in action, to see it multiply in their hands: to participate in something... with their God."

Argoth paused and took a sip of honey-ale to soothe his throat.

"You see Mr. James there is one thing that El hath given all; one thing unique to all men, and angels; one thing unique to those gifted with sentience... choice. And unlike some, I have known who Lucifer was *prior* to his fall. So no Mr. James; I would not have killed him. For, to do so would be to extinguish the goodness of God that at one time was manifested even through him. Moreover, who is Argoth? Am I *God,* Mr. James? Who would dare be God and take a life that God has created when the image of God stands before you in obedience to his creator? Your line of logic would have had El extinguish the human race Mr. James. For from the moment Adamson disobeyed: his path before him was set. As for me, I would be like the Lord; has God any pleasure that the wicked would die? And not that he should turn from his wicked ways and live? No, Mr. James I did not kill Lucifer; who was at *that* time *not* a thief who sought to kill, steal and destroy. He was not *always* Satan. But I digress. There is a reason I have brought you here. I have watched your Mr. James and have noted that you are also a Grigori of sorts.

And because of this affinity I will soon give you a gift that no human has ever been offered."

Henel was taken aback and replied, "What gift?"

Argoth looked Henel in the eye and replied. "The infinite gift of choices."

"I don't understand," said Henel.

Argoth took another sip of his tea and set it down on the side table near him. "You will Mr. James—in time you will."

* * *

Michael-Theta had called the Lumazi into the council chambers. Lilith stood to his right and the rest of the Lumazi sat themselves down.

"You know why I have called you all here?"

Gabriel of the Theta realm looked at Jerahmeel and Talus. Sariel eyed Michael and let out a large sigh. "Believe me when I say that we are anxious to learn why?"

Michael-Theta looked at Sariel and replied, "I am sure. Lucifer must be found. He must answer to the charges leveled against him. He must answer for the vision that the Grigori have leveled against him."

Gabriel-Theta eyed Lilith and spoke, "You mean *this* Grigori? For, prior to his coming no one had accused our brother of *anything*. Not even Raphael brought such an accusation. The Lord rebuke you Lilith from whatever realm you hail from: the Lord rebuke you!"

Jerahmeel-Theta placed his hands on Gabriel's shoulder to calm him. "Michael you told us that Raphael portaled Lucifer and another Grigori from Lilith's realm away. I very much would like to find them. For this other Grigori may be able to bear witness to the words of this one here. Or perhaps…" Jerahmeel then turned to look into Lilith's glowing eyes.

"…help determine if we are being deceived."

Gabriel rose up, and he bent over the table and glowered at Michael, "And what of the death of Raphael! What of the death of my brother?"

Michael also rose and placed his hand on the hilt of his sword.

Jerahmeel reached out to touch Gabriel and calm him. "The consequences of Raphael's death will be answered when El returns from Sabbath. Then of a surety our sins...both collective...," He then looked at Michael and Lilith in the eye when he spoke so that it was clear that Raphael's passing would not be forgotten. "... and individual will find us all out."

Michael nodded in understanding. *"If,* El awakens, but until then are we in agreement that they must be found?"

Talus-Theta spoke up, "Yes, Michael. But found and brought to trial... *not* executed. Know that you lead by consent of the Lumazi. You are *not* the appointed Chief Prince. And know that if Lucifer and this angel are not given a hearing; understand that I will not be a party to his death. Nor will house Arelim. The blood of Lucifer will not be on our hands."

The other heads of the angelic houses nodded. Gabriel also spoke and looked Michael squarely in the eye and pointed at his brother "He is *not* to be harmed Michael."

Michael nodded. "Understood, I will do my best brother but also understand that in the end, that will be dependent upon him."

The whole of the Lumazi then stood to their feet, and each proceeded to make their way out the meeting chamber.

"Well that went as well as could be expected." Lilith whispered.

Michael nodded, "Agreed, have you spoken with the other Grigori?"

Lilith bowed his cowled head. "Yes, the House considers the death of Raphael an internal matter and both Janus, Argoth and I are all in agreement. There is another Grigori that has entered the realm and has refused to submit to the order. It is imperative that he be found."

"And where has your search taken you to where Raphael has attempted to hide Lucifer?"

"There is but one place one can hide from a Grigori my prince: a null. There are few that would provide cover from our eyes and only one that we need explore."

"And the name of this place?" Michael asked.

"Eden, High Prince. We believe they reside on Earth near a null void in the region of Eden. Janus has agreed to send Argoth, and he has been dispatched with orders."

Michael turned to him confused and replied, "Orders? What will your brother do to the other Grigori?"

Lilith smiled but his features could not be made out by Michael from under the angel's cowl. But Lilith replied in the simplicity that marked his people.

"He will be redacted high prince."

"And what of Lucifer?" Michael asked.

"We both know what the vision has shown you. We both know what must be done."

Michael nodded reluctantly. "I know… I know."

Michael-Theta turned to face Lilith. "Come, and take me to your bounty hunter; for if my brother must die. Let it be by my own hand."

* * *

Argoth-Theta landed at Eden per instructions given to him by Janus-Theta. Eden was indeed a beautiful region. The pinnacle of floral beauty; Eden was the lush, tropical, and palatial home of the Lord's greatest creation. Argoth-Theta considered it unfortunate that Raphael had saw fit to bring the enemies of the kingdom to the world of the humans. The angel determined to be respectful of their domain and he would do his best to tread lightly as to not needlessly trespass. El's pronouncement was clear. The humans were to steward over this world. It was not meant to be given to angelic kind to call a home.

He ceased his observation of the forests before him and the blue skies above and turned his attention to the task at hand: to find Lilith Grigori.

He was a redactor now. Commissioned by his people to ferret out falsehood and it was time to get to work.

Argoth-Theta took from his robes an ink-horn and tossed it into the air. The black liquid emptied and floated into the air like a giant bubble. "Map of the region," he said aloud.

The ink then moved and laid out before him a three dimensional overview of a flat map showing the elevation of the whole of the Edenic region.

"Narrow the search parameters to known regional nulls."

Again the black ink floated and moved to redraw the area as commanded.

Two zones were now drawn in three dimensions and he took his stylus into his hand and twisted the reed between his fingers as he meditated on the two choices between him. He eyed each area and studied it as he spoke aloud to himself.

"Raphael, where did you teleport them and more importantly... why?"

The Grigori continued to eye the two options to begin his apprehension of Lilith-Theta and deal with this Grigori from another realm. He noted that one null was further from the garden where the Adam slept, nor did it serve as a priority for Grigoric oversight.

He spoke to the black ink, "Is there journaling in this region here?"

The black substance moved to and fro until it pulled back to one spot where Argoth was able to see through it.

He studied the region and then eyed his present location the more. He took his ink-horn and placed it in the palm of his hand. "Retract" he said.

Immediately the black liquid flowed into the container until it was seen no more and Argoth placed the ink-horn back within the folds of his robes.

His pen then turned into a dagger and floated near his face and he spoke to it. "Take me to him."

Immediately the blade shot off into the sky and Argoth-Theta ascended into the air to follow.

His hunt for his wayward brother had now begun.

* * *

Lilith-Theta noted Lucifer's wound was slowly healing. "He will recover," said Lilith. "But to your point earlier. I have given thought to your plan. Neither of us can portal the three of us to the gate."

Argoth sat on the grass floor of the jungle in which they dwelled, he lifted his knee and leaned upon it. "No," he said. "But if we join our powers together, we can transport us to the gate."

Argoth then rose to his feet and turned his ear to the sky. "The wind whispers that we are not alone."

A swishing sound was heard and Argoth's stylus instantly turned into a dagger and deflected what seemed like a blade that was but mere inches from his face. The angel backed up and Lilith also stood to his feet and his own stylus transformed into a dagger.

Another swish sounded as if something was cutting through the air quickly and the object moved and a ghostly figure appeared from between the trees and spoke.

"Thank you for speaking of your plan. I will see that Heaven is prepared to repel your advance."

Lilith cried out towards the figure. "Who goes there? And why do you sneak upon he who was appointed by the head of our House?"

Argoth-Theta laughed then replied. "Greetings, Lilith. I am here by command of our house. You are hereby accused to be in violation of Grigoric law and of giving sanctuary to a fugitive wanted by the Lumazi. You will surrender your tome or you will be redacted."

Argoth then looked at the cloaked figure and spoke in return. "He will not comply for he is under my protection. Leave us and I will not inflict harm upon you."

The Grigori looked up to gaze at Argoth. He eyed the angel and slowly lifted his hood to reveal his face and both angels could now clearly make out the features of the other. Each stared back at a face that was their own. Each one's dagger poised to be unleashed. Each eyed one another in disbelief: disbelief until they both muttered one phrase aloud as they stood but five yards from the other.

"In El's name."

* * *

Raphael entered Limbo expecting to see a host arrayed against him. Mentally prepared for battle, the head of House Grigori was armed to defend himself and set to find his lost friends. His tome buffered the realm against invasion, and it no longer resided within his chest. He was now bound by time. Limbo like Heaven was infinite, thus here was a realm where one could become lost; lost and unable to return to the shores of Heaven's comfort and familiarity. For Limbo was the flotsam of Time and the cast off of decisions not made. In this realm eternity's currents streamed and flowed through the land as storm surge; as the discarded choices of sentient beings now played out ad infinitum in Limbo. Here one could meet a version of oneself that was the remnant of a choice not made. Here in limbo, if not secured by an anchor one could potentially go… mad.

Limbo was a dangerous realm made off limits by God. A causeway created to prevent travel to Aseir. A reminder by the Creator that choice was a gift. And if El so chose — a quality that could be withdrawn by the Lord. In Limbo, evil itself could be explored and made real. There were many in Heaven that were oblivious of what lived inside this domain.

But Raphael knew.

Raphael understood that there were choices from the Host that now clamored for escape. Knew that in this dimension choices were made alive and deliberated how they would take physical form and replace choices already made in the prime realm.

Raphael was the seal of God's knowledge. He knew all of angelic kind could not appreciate what Limbo was nor understand that it was the volitional septic tank of choices discarded; the land of predestination and the county that cradled the mystery that was free will.

And here within the same he now clamored in the foggy murk that he might find and rescue his stranded friends. For Raphael moved through the dimness and cloudy land. Great ornate columns towered in the twilight; monoliths that testified to the work when El had built Heaven's foundation. Here in this… wilderness could those choices that displeased El be released into the wasteland: a wilderness that led to several places. The Maelstrom, Aseir, and a nether realm of fire El had cordoned off even before he had placed barriers in the way to Aseir. A land lit in fire and brimstone: a volca-nic region unknown to all but the Sephiroth. A place God had pre-pared; a breathing thing that seemingly was alive yet stood waiting for the call to *be*; waiting to be unleashed and crafted into something more. But for now it was buried deep in preservation for a future Raphael was unsure. The angel wondered if the burning lands of Aseir if ever unleashed would harm those not given authority to experience the heat from the living flame.

And he realized that he did not desire to find out.

Raphael floated onward and he could hear in the distance the roars of the Zoa.

Heaven's scavengers that fed off the discards of sentient choices: creatures that fed off... the Mists.

Zoa were scavengers that ate all things discarded by Heav-en: the consumers of all Heaven's refuse. Their presence along with the Mists, and the ever changing landscape of Heaven made travel through Limbus perilous. After the Schism the Lord removed the barriers that kept the creatures at bay.

Raphael quietly moved through Limbo looking for the echo of his friends. Reverberations of their journals would ping his tome. And like the vibrations of a spider's web he was sensitive to the

Grigoric heartbeat that resonated from the volumes of his people. It would take time, lack of interference from the Mists and Zoa, but they could be found and retrieved. Yet, the barrier he created in front of Jerahmeel would not hold forever. He only had so long before the barricade was destroyed and the Prime realm was open to Limbo.

He lifted his hands above his eyes as dust and particulate matter flew into his face and a great wind rushed through the large cavern within which he flew.

A crackle of energy erupted over head and a temporal storm appeared near the great caverns ceiling and powerful reality changing winds suddenly howled about him. Their gallop was such that the breeze entered crevices and the cut outs of walls made the grottos sing in a whistle like fashion. Raphael noted that even here in the depths of the basement of Heaven did Heaven carol of the glory of God. For within the depth of fog that ran the length of this dreary land. God's power and majesty was still etched in each column and ran the length and breadth of the towering ceilings.

Plasma burst all about him as lightning arced in crackling tentacles that stretched across both floor and ceiling. A major decision had taken place in the prime realm and the discarding of all others flowed into Limbo as sheets of torrential rain. The sparks of lightning scraped against the floor as a match-strike and ignited small fires; fires that created the creatures known as the Mists.

Vaporous humanoid clouds rose from the ground, and as they rose; a female sounding shriek rose with them; blood-curdling screams of rage and anger that echoed from being discarded. Abandoned choices deposited in the land of Heaven that were now gaining life... and consciousness: a consciousness that was birthed in fire, pain, and screams.

Mist-like beings that rose as a foggy army to understand they were the shed skin of those who were gifted with volition.

Beings now awakened that turned their heads to see that a living creature of volition walked among their midst--- Raphael.

Raphael stopped his advanced as he became slowly surrounded by the newly birthed clouds of anger. He kept himself still to not provoke the creatures, for the Mists were eager to possess and consume choice; to cause one to bend their will towards enslavement to sin.

The temporal storm continued unabated. It's fury untempered as it passed along the lid of the basement of Heaven. The circling tornadic gale continued to unleash a bevy of arc discharges that caged Raphael from advancing further even if he was so inclined.

The temporal storm's path made the ground and all about him appear then disappear. Each bolt that stuck the ground heaved stones into the air causing them to float. Boulders and granite platforms phased into existence then phased out again. Each boulder solidifying then vanishing in orbit around the ground where lightning struck.

The storm continued its march across the paved stones and moved forward and it advanced deeper into the darkness; following a path that all the storms in this realm followed: a path towards the Nexus.

The center of Limbus and the seat of Limbo's god appointed ruler… Lotan.

Lotan was the Mist King: the center of Limbo's convergence and the prince assigned to this territory by El.

The newly formed clouds of forsaken choices continued their formation and stood as a growing army of foggy infantry with yellow eyes.

Each temporal bolt of the storm illuminated the giant columns that towered above. Bridges that crossed ancient and deep chasms collapsed as the localized typhoon passed overhead and its voltaic fury discharged lightning strikes in all directions. And with each blast the Mists were birthed and their screams echoed across the cavern.

Raphael then understood why he had not encountered his perceived enemy; cognizant why none attacked him. He watched as the mists lifted their heads as if something moved in the darkness. None suddenly seemed to care for his presence as all suddenly began to disperse. Giant wings and tentacled creatures fell from the cavern above him. Roars that signaled that the Zoa hunted and they inhaled the shrieking cries of the Mist. Raphael too began to fly away chasing after the storm he could still see in the dimness ahead of him: a storm that followed the drainage path through Limbo: a path that led to Lotan.

Raphael scurried past giant tentacles that flailed about him: tentacles with gnashing mouths that inhaled the foggy humanoids into their large orifices. Raphael stayed solid resisting the urge to phase as a gas lest he too succumb to the vacuumed hungers of the beasts. The giant winged octopi seemed to ignore him; caught up in the frenzy that was the newly formed mists that scattered as antelope under attack from a pack of lions.

Suddenly the air became charged and the sound of howling winds filled the immediate area and light flashed above his head and Raphael saw that another temporal storm now raged around him. Howls, voices and bolts of lightning flared out in all directions. The eye of the storm opened and he could see that all of house Grigori seemed to march into Limbo and at their head, Janus led them. A thunderbolt stuck behind him and Raphael turned to see that the Zoa had dispersed in fear of the storm. And those Mists not consumed by the Zoa were sucked up into the whirlwind of the storm and Raphael also looked to see where he could hide from the now constant bombardment of electrified limbs. Explosions ripped around him and instinctively he misted and in the same instant was struck by an arm of the storm.

He cried out in agony as the current ripped through his body and the angel became paralyzed unable to move. Like a fly caught in a web he was suspended in a lattice of heated arcs that moved as spider legs across the cavern floor. Legs that corralled him and that prevented his escape: slowly the storm began to churn deeper into the cavern: the tempests trajectory now echoing the earlier cyclones that had come before.

Temporal power ripped through his frame and he gritted his teeth in a vain attempt to endure the agony that now wracked his jerking and spasmodic body. Current flowed through his misted person and he felt himself being torn apart. Images and flashes of locales lined the wall of the ribbons of rain and flashes of settings were revealed to his eyes: squadrons of angels.

Armies marched through Limbo as well as instances of his own past, present and future materialized before him and the angel screamed in agony.

His screams now part of the ambiance that was Limbo. For Raphael, in undefinable pain was now tossed about as a unit of storm debris that lanced the ground and ceiling as the cyclone marched towards its unknown destination. And the chief prince of house Grigori was taken; helpless to escape from the grasp of the storms voltaic grip.

* * *

Argoth distrusted the face that stared back at him—distrusted it because what stared back at him was naught but the mirror of his own. And the thought unnerved him.

He stepped in a cautious circling stride of his double; both angels wary of one another, both with daggers drawn.

"This is a trick." Argoth-Theta said.

"No my friend," said Argoth. "Not a trick. But it is true that I am neither of your world; nor you from mine. But I *am* here to apprehend he who we both know is *also,* not of this world. Help me find and detain him, and I will be on my way."

"The decision to bind the time-traveler is not mine to give. But this one does fall under my purview." Argoth-Theta pointed at Lilith. "This one here is required to surrender his tome and stylus and appear before House Grigori for judgment."

Lilith-Theta looked at his approaching peer and stood over the unconscious Lucifer-Theta to protect him. "I will not comply. For, I am here on command of Raphael Grigori the head of our house. The Chief Prince also falls under my protection and neither of them has given order that I am to do as you require. You are executing an illegal order and have thought more of thyself than you ought to think. I repeat — I will not comply."

Argoth-Theta then looked at his twin and replied, "And what of you? Will you hinder my order to seize this one? Even as you seek *me* to assist *you?* Will *you* also defy House Grigori when it commands accountability from one of its own members? Tell me, do you mirror the heart of the Grigori to obey when our House gives command? Or do you simply mirror my face?"

Argoth nodded his head. "I have both heard and seen what the Head of House Grigori of this realm willed towards this one here. I have *also* spoken to the Chief Prince. I cannot stand idle and allow you to obstruct the order of the Lord. Lucifer is Chief Prince, and unless El states otherwise, there is no law in existence that will undo that. Go thy way, for you do not know the spirit with which you move. For, thou art aligned in usurpation and have strayed from the way. Let us be. Be warned and know that if thy choice is to enforce this illegal order it shall lead thee towards conflict, and I stand as Redactor of our House and I will not be defied." Argoth then took from his robes two dual bladed daggers and held each in his hands. Dual blades extended from both ends of the weapons. He then took a shield guard stance and squatted slightly to the ready.

Argoth-Theta nodded in understanding and replied, "Then you shall be defied."

He too revealed a dagger and his stance was in the high guard, and the dagger which he unsheathed floated above him weaving back and forth in the air like a cobra poised ready to strike.

Lilith-Theta also pulled out his dagger, and he too took a high guard stance and gave warning. "Approach the Chief Prince or myself and know that dissolution awaits you."

Argoth-Theta then approached Argoth and slowly placed his right foot over his left as the two circled one another as two leopards ready to pounce, and each slowly moved away from Lilith and Lucifer.

"Lilith, take the Chief Prince to where we discussed, and I will follow. Go now and do as I say."

Argoth-Theta then let his dagger fly towards Argoth while he himself ran towards Lilith.

Argoth parried the blade that flew as a dart towards his face.

Lilith attacked Argoth-Theta with a downward stroke and the angel let the blade pass through him and then rematerialized to grasp at the angel's throat.

The floating dagger of Lilith then turned back towards its foe and counter-attacked and it pierced the angel's bicep plunging through the same arm that held Lilith by the throat, and Argoth-Theta let out a scream.

Argoth continued to parry the self-attacking blade that accosted him and with his own double bladed daggers, deflected the knife of his opponent back towards him.

Argoth-Theta gritted his teeth as the knife of Lilith twisted on its own accord, ripping through muscle in the angel's arm.

And Lilith, thinking the angel defenseless, did not see the deflected blade that flew towards him until it was too late, and the dagger that was deflected by Argoth slashed his face.

Lilith screamed and his scream woke the Chief Prince from his slumber; and when Lucifer eyed the attacking Argoth-Theta. He opened his mouth and unleashed a roar. Argoth-Theta looked up and released his grip on Lilith and phased. But the visible and conical force wave expanded as it traveled and slammed into the phased Grigori and sent him careening into the forest. The trunks of trees and giant branches exploded into splinters. Others snapped and fell from the forest roof top and Lilith and Lucifer watched as a cathedral of towering trees and vines rained down crashing upon the repelled angel.

Lilith's dagger then immediately flew to its master and settled above him in a defensive position.

Lucifer turned his head and spoke to Argoth, "It would seem that we are found."

Creaking and the crackling and snapping of trees could be heard as if some giant lumbered through the forest, and a white light lit the area and Lucifer barked to the duo, "Get behind me now!"

Each did as commanded and when they did the trees disintegrated before them in a flash of prismatic light. And when the explosive light abated; Michael stood with several of his Arelim guards and Argoth-Theta stood by his side.

Argoth and Lilith closed ranks behind Lucifer and the two touched hands and spoke angel speak. Immediately, a blue portal opened behind them and Lilith grabbed Lucifer's collar and pulled him through and Argoth turned to follow. The portal began to close and Argoth-Theta misted and he sprinted after them and also floated into the vanishing portal, and the quartet disappeared in a flash of prismatic light.

Michael and the guards were left alone on the edge of Eden and he commanded them saying. "Lilith has made an error for they have revealed where they seek to hide. For the portal displayed the pillars resident in the basement of Heaven. Come... there is but one place they intend to flee. Now go to and assemble a squadron of twelve of Heaven's finest to apprehend those who have absconded away. For they seek to escape the immediate jurisdiction of Jerusalem and seek to travel into Limbus; they think that I will not follow. They are wrong. When thou hast done as I have asked, meet me at the Gate of Limbus and tell Gabriel that he is in command of Heaven. For, I must depart to traverse the realm and hunt these that have escaped."

Each of the three angels lifted their fists in unison to their chests in salute to Michael and they looked up and prismatic clouds surrounded them and they were gone.

Michael slowly surveyed the sight of where Lucifer and his companions had laid their heads to rest, and he examined the forest floor and noted the blood-marked area of depressed leaves that was used for bedding. He bent down and touched it and felt its consistency within his fingers. He raised it to his nose to smell it and then lifted the tip of his finger to his tongue. The angel of the Lord then smiled and nodded knowingly. He stood up and spoke the Elomic command to open a ladder and was gone in twinkling prismatic light.

* * *

A portal opened in the basement of Heaven and Lilith-Theta, Lucifer-Theta and Argoth emerged.

"Get down!" Argoth ordered. A dagger whizzed over the three angels and each moved to escape its deadly blade. Lilith misted and Lucifer armored before the blade could pierce his skin.

The edge nicked his shoulder but left but a scratch upon his hardened exterior. The white gate shimmered and before the portal closed the misted Argoth Theta floated through the collapsing gateway and approached his namesake.

"Lilith do as I command... now!" ordered Argoth.

Lilith turned towards Lucifer who was loath to leave, and Lilith eyed the Chief Prince and spoke. "Our hopes rest on you. Into the gate my prince, please!"

Lucifer frowned and Lilith took his hand and both he and the angel hurriedly flew into the blue Gate of Limbus and disappeared.

Argoth alone stood before the gate to cover their escape and when he saw that they had departed he moved to close ranks with his twin, de-misted and engaged his double in hand to hand combat.

190

Argoth-Theta met his equal, and the two blocked and parried blow after blow. In a style of combat similar to martial arts they lifted their legs to block kicks, and each entangled the other yet neither gaining an advantage.

When one would create an opening to strike, the other would close it just as quickly. Knife hand strikes were opposed by forearm blocks and back fist blows landed to non-effect as the two misted and materialized as fast as each assailed one another. Each was a blur with daggers striking in the air, with Argoth's-Theta's single dagger able to fend off the duo blades of Argoth.

Each fought relentlessly one another to a stalemate: until there was not.

An entourage of angels made their way down the stairs to the basement of Heaven and leading them with Michael and not far behind him was Janus-Theta.

Janus upon seeing the skirmish flung his dagger at Argoth. Argoth weaved and ducked to keep himself from being slashed. Argoth viewed the scene and realizing that the numbers were no longer in his favor disengaged from battle with Argoth-Theta and turned to escape. He leaped into the portal as multiple daggers flew after him; each disappeared into the blue gate that was Limbo; each following their target through the dimensional barrier.

Argoth opened his palm, and the blade returned floating to his side and he set himself to follow until Michael spoke out.

"Hold Argoth, come and let us take council before we pursue."

"But my prince," Argoth replied, "Limbo ever shifts. We must hurry before they escape into the lands of mist."

"They will not escape," assured Michael. "There is no place Lucifer can go that I will not follow. No place can he run that I shall not pursue."

Michael then looked to his Arelim soldiers and pointed at the glowing gate into Limbo. "To remove the stalemate that exists between thee and thy dimensional twin, we will go together my friend. When we are united, there are none that can stop the Host. Now walk with me and let us proceed, to bring them to justice, to bring the rebel who would launch a war against God back alive."

Michael, Argoth, Janus-Theta and twelve Arelim soldiers then marched into the gleaming blue gate into Limbus. An angelic band of bounty hunters determined to seize their prize.

Lucifer had assembled his armies outside the plateau that approached the gate of Argoth. Eladrin was now settled upon the pad that ladders regularly descended and his people had suspended all traffic into Heaven using that approach. For the King of Ophanim now sat upon the mountain and his rings were open wide, gyrating to and fro as volts of plasma arched across the causeway. A portal of portals that would swallow armies' whole did the King of Ladders now make; and before him was assembled the Host of Heaven: a legion of angels of mixed houses. Angels massed to contend with the seceded house that was Grigori. A house that had in their audacity dared to break with the council of angels, and themselves leave the golden city of Jerusalem to follow an impostor into Limbo; an angel not of their own realm. Lucifer stood before the throng of soldiers. A multitude equipped with both spear and shield. And with his hand the Chief Prince waved his army forward. And by his command the military might of Heaven marched as bidden; thousands upon a thousand thousands marched through the body of Eladrin into Limbo.

Thus, the realm of Limbo strained and swelled to contain Heaven's invasion. Her boundaries fattened by the souls of angelic legions that now marched upon her ephemeral shores: a tripartite army that would wage war within her coalescent mists.

To be continued...

Grigoric Glossary of Terms

El or Jehovah

The name angels have given to God and by which He has revealed Himself to them. Triune in nature, El is often seen in a singular bodily form. On rare occasions, His triune nature is revealed as three separate distinct personalities (Father, Son, and Holy Ghost); collectively they are called the Godhead.

Elohim

The collective name of all celestial kind in Biblical lore; also called the Sons of God. Elohim are distinct from Yeshua, who is the only Begotten Son. Let it be known that Grigoric trances have shown that righteous men will also be adopted into the family of God. This knowledge is not yet commonly known among the people.

The Schism

An event in Heavenly history that caused the separation of the three celestial races, attributed to Lucifer's trafficking to elevate the Elohim above the Ophanim and Seraphim.

The Descension

The day noted by all angelic kind that Lucifer was thrown out of Heaven.

Godhead

The Trinity composed of the Father (El), the Son (Yeshua), and the Holy Ghost (El Pneuma).

Chief Prince

An honorific title given to one of seven angelic princes who stands before the presence of God and receives instructions for his race. The Chief Prince is entrusted by El to walk within the Stones of Fire and to protect the secret of the chamber, the Primestone, which is a repository of God's power where one may become as God. Michael stands as Chief Prince of Angels. Lucifer formerly held this rank. This rank is not to be confused with the Angel of the Lord, who is Yeshua.

Lumazi (Re 4:5)

The group of seven archangels who stand before the throne of God. They are the chief angelic council that executes the will of God in the universe. The head of each major house is represented on the council. The seven houses are Malakim, Kortai, Draco, Issi, Arelim, Grigori, and Harrada.

Ladder (AKA Orphanic Portal) (Ge 28:12)

A mode of transport utilized by angels to travel between realms. Ladders are created by the Ophanim. Angels simply travel in the wake that the celestial beings create as they move from place to place.

Limbo or Limbus

Also known as the Realm of Choices; an in-between place. The land between life and death. The land of infinite possibilities. Limbo is placed in the basement of Heaven, yet above the Maelstrom of the Abyss. It is the only passage to the other side of the Mountain of God that leads to the land of the Seraphim, as well as to other regions of Heaven.

Tartarus (2 Peter 2:4)

A prison designed by Lucifer to dispose of those who opposed him. Presently it is in use by the Lord as a holding cell until He has determined their end.

Ashe

The legendary city of fire and home of the Seraphim. A metropolis made of living fire. The city is located in the land of Aseir.

Hell

A living mountain that serves as a prison. Designed originally with angels in mind, it lives off the eternal spirit of Elomic flesh. It possesses the ability to reproduce similar to an amoeba and can grow. Grigoric spies indicate that Hell has grown to hold captive humans. (Isa 5:14 Therefore hell hath enlarged herself, and opened her mouth without measure: and their glory, and their multitude, and their pomp, and he that rejoiceth, shall descend into it.)

Scouts indicate that humans now abide in two compartments within the creature. Hades: the realm of the unrighteous dead. Paradise: The realm of the righteous dead. Prior to Yeshua's resurrection, Paradise was the place where the righteous dead were held in the spirit realm until they were freed. These two domains were separated by a gulf that prevented residents from crossing to one another. (Luke 16:26)

Shiloah

The title angels have given the man who can defeat Lucifer.

Dissolution

"Death" to a celestial being is called dissolution.

The Kiln

A furnace from which El created all celestial life and the former storehouse of the Stones of Fire; the living elements of creation. At the heart of the Kiln was the Primestone, and the ultimate test for angelic kind.

Elomic Command

A vowel, consonant, or phrase allowing the power of God to be invoked.

The Abyss

A gulf of nether sometimes referred to by thy kind as Limbo or by daemon kind as "the wilderness." It is a realm that separates the Third and Second Heavens. Failure to bridge the realms without a Ladder or direct intervention from El can cause one to be entrapped within the winds of the nether.

The winds are referred to as the Maelstrom. Kortai builders frequently built near the edge of the Maelstrom to expand the landscape of Heaven. The Abyss is also referred to as the "bottomless pit."

Mortals cannot pass through the Abyss without shedding their corporeal shell. Only Death or direct translation by God allows passage past the Abyss into the spiritual world of Heaven. El hath mentioned that He may release this tome to thee at a later time.

Waypoint

A designated area where travel between two points was allowed by God. Failure to utilize a waypoint could displace the Third Heaven with the second or vice versa causing untold destruction.

Grigoric Trance

A vision given by God to some Grigori who are able on occasion to see one generation ahead into the future.

Manna

The food that angels consume. Grown in the fields of Elysium, it is shipped to the four corners of creation to supply angels with sustenance. When harvested, it instantly grows back. During the exodus of the children of Israel, the nation temporarily fed on this food. (Exodus 16:15)

Cadmime/cadmium

A black crystal-like mineral created by God. It is a living thing that grows similar to human bones. It is the hardest, most durable substance known to angelic kind. The substance is used to undergird the basement of heaven and her foundations. It can stretch and grow as directed. It is extremely pliable and able to be made into a variety of substances from building materials to weapons of war.

The Burning

The Burning is a process that the Seraphim may engage where all Seraphim may unite as one single entity. All who participate while in this state are able to know and share one another's thoughts.

Their collective flame is equivalent to the flames of Hell or the former Kiln. There are few things that can survive if the collective body of Seraphim fires.

Creatures

Cherubim

A type of angel having great power; but not necessarily governmental oversight.

Seraphim

A heavenly creature designed to serve as a voice to the holiness of God; also called a "Burning One." A creature of great power.

There are four which stand at the temple of God. The rest of the Seraphim have not been seen since the great Schism and are kept behind the mountain of God in the land of Aseir.

The Seraphim appear as floating fire with flaming eyes and wings in their natural state and assume a humanoid form when in the presence of others. When they do so, their voices can create sounds that defy the hearing. El hath restricted full access to their tome.

Virtue

A living sentient aroma that lives before the throne of God and perfumes the throne. El hath restricted full access to their tome.

Ophanim (Ezekiel 1:15-21)

A heavenly creature designed to serve as a guard to the presence of God. They are also movers of planetary and star systems. El hath restricted full access to their tome.

Zoa (Rev. 4:1-9 5:1- 6:1)

A heavenly creature designed to serve as a guard to the secret things of God.

Stones of Fire (Eze 28:14)

A living sentient element which can be molded in the Kiln to create celestial life. They are also called Kilnstones or Godstones.

Shekinah Glory

The residue of God's breath, equivalent to the exhaling of a human's carbon dioxide; a living cloak of breathing light that envelops and irradiates the person of God. Primarily, a localized phenomenon. Those that come near the Lord are irradiated by the Shekinah, leaving an afterglow on their own person for a temporary period. The Shekinah can manifest wherever the holiness and righteousness of God exist.

Aithon

The famed flaming horses of Aseir. These great animals pull the fiery chariots of Seraphim riders and were the steeds used to bring Elijah into Heaven. Those that are tamed are stalled in the great flaming city of Ashe.

Angelic Rankings

Chief Prince

El's designated angelic leader over all Elohim

The First of Angels/The Sum of all Things (Ez 28:12,13)

An honorific title given to Lucifer

High Prince

Seven angels in existence who speak collectively for all their kind. (Collectively, they are called the Lumazi and are sometimes referred to individually with that honorific title.)

Archon

A sole high-ranking governing angel who directs a specific assignment or regions of territory (s). Sometimes referred to by humans as archangels. The highest-ranking angel over an assignment.

Principality

A sole mid-ranking governing angel who administers more than one territory.

Powers

The lowest ranking governing angel overseeing one territory.

Prime

A non-governing angel representative of a particular virtue. (I.e., love, justice, etc.) After the fall, some angels were designated as prime evils.

Minister

A non-governing angel who serves the cause of El

Daemon

A fallen non-governing angel who serves the cause of Lucifer. Daemons are the regurgitated angelic souls of Hell, released by he who holds the keys to Death and Hell.

Daemons are but shadows of their former angelic selves and thrive off men, as their Kilnstones have been digested by Hell. Now they seek to inhabit the souls of men, that they might find expression through them.

Specter

Fallen Grigori sometimes referred to by humans as Ghosts.

Shaun-tea'll

A group of angelic warrior dispatched to dispense the judgment of the Lord

The Great Angelic Houses of Heaven

House Draco: Sigil: A dragon

House Draco is the first house of angels and is considered to be highborn in the angelic cast. All Draco are angels of praise and represent beauty, wisdom, and art. Lucifer, prior to his fall, was their represented leader and the first-born of all angels.

Each Draco has within him the ability to generate sound; some Draco are specifically limited to areas of sound. For example, some Draco can generate all notes within the soprano range, others in the tenor, bass, and alto, but they cannot generate sounds outside the range created. Lucifer is not so and can create any sound.

All Draco have a shimmering translucent skin that allows them to reflect light and therefore project images. They can project certain wavelengths of the spectrum. Each Draco is unique in that they are limited to certain areas of the spectrum. Lucifer, as their leader, is not so limited and may project any image. He may even disappear from view if he chooses, to cloak himself in light and be invisible to the eye.

Metatron has now succeeded Lucifer as Prince of his people. Draco, when they choose to be visible to humans, reveal themselves as winged serpents.

Harrada: Sigil: An owl

The House Harrada are considered great sages of wisdom and lore, meticulous in their desire to create order and excel in the development of systems management and the written word.

Each member of house Harrada is adept at manipulating the elements, including heat, air, water, and earth. Also known as lovers of writing, they often create great literary works. Jerahmeel represents the embodiment of the Harrada. Prior to the Descension, God used Jerahmeel to temper Lucifer's tendency toward arrogance.

Harada are keepers of order within all three realms of creation and also exercise control over time and seasons. Harrada is often the head or manager of Heaven's day-to-day operations, including the harvesting of manna. Other angels of this house include Zeus and Chronos.

Kortai: Sigil: A Hammer

The Kortai is a race of builders, muscular and adept in the manipulation of metallurgy and woodworking, minerals and gems. They are the ultimate engineers and constructors of Heaven. Curious to a fault, they have no qualms about delving into new architectural endeavors. It was the Kortai that volunteered to work against the Maelstrom to expand Heaven.

Kortai have a youthful appearance and are incredibly strong in spite of their smaller stature. The Kortai are the engineers of Heaven and are able to bring into creation whatever can be conceived. Michael the archangel is the leader of this house. Since the war, they carry a hammer on one side of their belt and a sword in the other, ready to either build or fight at a moment's notice.

Assumably, all that left Heaven did so out of outright rebellion, but those Kortai that left went to see something new, thinking that more than what El had shown them existed, and they were moved to build something apart from El's designs. These are the builders of the Hell forge and the deep chasms that run throughout Hell. Lucifer has silently been turning the Kortai into daemons.

Grigori: Sigil: Two Eyes, a flame, an inkhorn, and stylus

The Grigori are chroniclers: They see all and record all. There are those who chronicle on behalf of God and those who chronicle on behalf of Satan. At least one Grigori records for God at all times. The watchers strive for perfection when documenting the events of history, but regardless of how they view God, their only motive is to chronicle as God designed them this way.

Those who chronicle for Satan say God's actions were not justified and therefore deserves to be overthrown. In the end, they believe their efforts will vindicate their belief in Satan's cause. They give commentary and chronicle with bias, or with an agenda that attempts to besmirch God. They do not simply chronicle...they editorialize. Their purpose for being is to compose. They may not, however, interfere with that which they behold. Those who attempt to harm them are themselves harmed. The Chief Prince is the exception, as he is embodied with authority and power over all angels.

Grigori cannot be stopped nor interfered with with-

213

out penalty of Abyssian or Tartarus confinement. They can interact with their own kind.

Grigori do not possess the common instruments associated with sight and hearing as they are naturally blind and deaf. They can see as well as anyone and can hear equally well, but they can see nothing but El. They hover, cloaked in purple hoods, and no one has ever seen their face. They have immunity from harm and are able to move freely within both spheres of engagement.

Formerly, Raphael was the prince that oversaw this house but was killed by the fall of Kilnstones during the civil war. Argoth is now the Chief of Eyes and Sephiroth of his house. A few of the Grigori have been gifted with the 'sight', the ability to see beyond what is written to that which shall be written. El has limited this ability; thus, Grigori can only see one generation ahead. When the Grigori use this ability, they go into a trance-like state and attempt to articulate the visions they see.

When El gives a prophecy to a prophet, He speaks to the prophet and allows the Grigori that shadows him to see ahead in time. Angels from this house include Argoth,

Hadriel, and Lilith, prior to his dissolution.

Arelim: Sigil: A bull's face

Arelim are strong angels who have the faces of bulls and cloven feet. They can be extremely aggressive in that they enjoy forms of competition. Highly driven by order and authority, yet always seeking to be first in every endeavor, they constantly use their great powers to move planets and power suns.

Able to manipulate the forces of gravity, El has used them to fling planets and keep orbits. Headed by Talus, many of those that left to follow Lucifer were of this house. Proud and strong, they comprise over half of Lucifer's force, making his numbers, though smaller than Heaven, equally formidable in power, for in his ranks reside some of the most powerful of angels. Other angels from this house include Apollyon AKA Abaddon, Marduk, and Sasheal

Issi: Sigil: A butterfly

Issi are lovers of beauty and their gifts allow one to touch anything and manipulate its color. They are also creatures of light, typically soft-spoken, they are humanoid yet prefer to be in touch with creation and typically morph into creatures such as Pegasi, unicorns, and even satyrs.

Able to mimic all life, they, like the Harrada and Draco, contribute to the culture of Heaven through their paintings and works of art. Gifted in tailoring and the beautification of one's physical form, their beauty is such that even Lucifer takes notice. When in their humanoid form, Issi possess wings similar to a butterfly. Sariel was the former Prince but sacrificed himself to expose the vulnerability of Abaddon. Azaziel now stands as Prince of his people.

The Issi also excels at all levels of herbalism and have now become healers as a result of the war. Issi can summon great celestial forces and target their enemies when in battle. Other angels from this house include Ashtaroth and Iblis.

Malakim: Sigil: Winged Feet

The angelic order of house Malakim are the messengers of God. If the Grigori are the eyes, the Malakim are its nerves. They constantly move to and fro throughout the realm delivering messages from various groups and ministers to one another. Like the Grigori in their numbers, they are similar in that they keep Heaven's communication lines open.

The Malakim ride steeds called gryphons. Each angel has a steed that is actually obtained when they acquire their first assignment from their Prince. Only the Chief Prince, the Grigori, and the House are aware of the celestial home of the Gryphons. Able to move at incredible speeds, they are the fastest of all angelic kind. Gabriel, who is their leader, is the fastest and wisest. It is rumored that his speed rivals that of the Ophanim.

This has yet to be tested. All Malakim have wings on their feet and not on their shoulders as others of their kind. Malakim actually run, but their speed is so fast that they appear to fly. Malakim can also manipulate lightning.

Articles of War

When El exiled the Horde to the nether, He then placed within the Kilnstones of all angelic kind His law that restricts the actions of our people. The following is understood by all Elohim concerning Elomic intervention in the affairs of men:

1. All souls are the Lords.

2. There shall be no interbreeding between species.

3. Humans shall not be brought into knowledge of your presence except through prayer or by voluntary submission to sin or by permission from El.

4. Agents of Lucifer may influence to their own ends human activity that humans, have submitted themselves to, or through affairs of those who possess spiritual authority have yielded themselves to.

5. Members of the Host will not invoke the powers of the enemy nor seek to drive and use powers apart from El's design. Doing so will constitute a rebellion and those who do so will be marked as members of the Horde.

6. The ruling powers over a household, region or power will be held responsible for all those under their charge.

7. Any officer who shall presume to muster a human as a soldier (who is not a soldier) shall be deemed guilty of having made a false muster and shall suffer accordingly.

The Shaun-tea'll will monitor the terms of these articles among both host and horde and shall have the power to imprison within Tartarus all who break them.

Thank You

Thank you for sharing in this fantasy series with me. More books are coming and I hope you will continue to follow my journeys. If you loved the book and would like to be informed of other books, please make sure you sign up to my mailing list here.

Feel free to leave a review!

Your help in spreading the word is gratefully appreciated and reviews make a huge difference in helping new readers find the series.

God bless you and I hope to see you within the pages of the next book!

Remember… there will be more stories so sign up for the mailing list!

About the Author

A lover of thought and the Bible, the Art of War and gaming; Donovan works professionally in the Human Services area and has a Master's degree in Nonprofit Management. He has over 20 years of service to the Christian community teaching the Bible as a member of the ordained clergy. Now retired from the clergy, Donovan has taken up his pen to express what has long been the untapped call God has placed in him to reach people through fiction.

Donovan's heart for ministry has carried into his secular pursuits and he has worked with countless abused and neglected children, adults with developmental disabilities, and women who have been victimized by domestic and sexual abuse. He has taught as an adjunct professor for several years and currently works full-time to end hunger in his local community.

Donovan has three adult children: Candace, Christopher, and Alexander. He currently resides in Michigan with his wife Lynnette.

Made in the USA
Coppell, TX
20 November 2020